The Digest Enthusiast

Book Eleven

Steve Carper

Peter Enfantino

Alfred Klosterman

John Kuharik

Janice Law

Gary Lovisi

Paul D. Marks

Rick McCollum

Marc Myers

Michael Neno

Vince Nowell, Sr.

Ward Smith

Bob Vojtko

Jeff Vorzimmer

Joe Wehrle, Jr.

Edited by Richard Krauss

The Digest Enthusiast (TDE) Book Eleven
Published twice a year by Larque Press LLC

Editor/Designer: Richard Krauss
Cover: Madame Selina by Rick McCollum
Cartoon: Bob Vojtko (page 57)
Photo: Duke Morse (page 150)

Printed on demand from Jan. 2020 in the United States of America
and other countries.

Larque Press LLC
4130 SE 162nd Court
Vancouver, WA 98683

Visit <larquepress.com> for news about current digest magazines and vintage digest
covers. Join our mailing list for exclusive updates on *The Digest Enthusiast* and other
Larque Press projects. Sign up at <larquepress.com>

Back Cover Images
Satellite Science Fiction Vol. 2 No. 1 Oct. 1957
Manhunt Detective Story Monthly Vol. 2 No. 11 Dec. 25, 1954
Alfred Hitchcock Mystery Magazine April 2015
Ellery Queen Mystery Magazine Sep/Oct 2017
Homicide Hotel Phantom Books No. 500
Astounding Science Fiction Nov. 1943

Our thanks to our contributors for some of the cover images that appear in this edition.
Cover images are retouched to remove defects from the original source material. When
reference material is not available, retouched areas are "best guess." In some cases text may
be reset in a font similar to the original work.

Opposite: Digests sharing the newsstand with the debut issue of
Michael Shayne Mystery Magazine in September 1956:
Homicide Detective Story Magazine No. 1
Murder Vol. 1 No. 1
Mercury Mystery Book Magazine Vol. 2 No. 7 (No. 220)
Manhunt Vol. 4 No. 9

The Digest Enthusiast
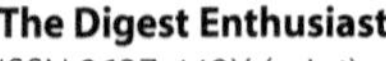
ISSN 2637-448X (print)
ISSN 2637-4498 (Kindle)
ISBN 978-1-7344548-0-2

ANHUNT
BEST SELLING CRIME-FICTION MAGAZINE
Murder!
KILL A WIFE
by
Lionel White
Mercury Mystery
BOOK MAGAZINE
EPITAPH
for a Virgin
by ROBERT ARTHUR
HOMICIDE
DETECTIVE STORY MAGAZINE
Sensational murder
mysteries by the top
crime story writers
OP, LOOK
D DIE
mystery
MacDONALD
Stories by —
JACK RITCHIE
RICHARD DEMING

News Digest

Analog Jan/Feb 2020

Analog Mar/Apr 2020

Congratulations to **Jackie Sherbow** and **Emily Hockaday**, both are now Managing Editors of Dell's mystery and science fiction books, respectively. Both are now supported by **Rae Purdom**, who has taken on the role of editorial administrative assistant at Dell Magazines. Rae is a graduate of Hampshire College, where he studied creative writing and media studies with a focus on speculative fiction.

Emily Hockaday: Analog

"*Analog Science Fiction and Fact* is celebrating their 90th year with the January/February 2020 issue, which features a throwback cover design and a retrospective reprint and editorial. Both the design and the reprint/editorial feature will appear for all 2020 issues.

"Coming up this year *Analog* will be featuring a new novel of **Derek Künsken's**—'The House of Styx'—along with exciting tales from **Neal Asher**, **Tom Jolly**, **Maggie Clark**, **Marie Vibbert**, **Adam-Troy Castro**, **Ramona Louise Wheeler**, and **Stanley Schmidt**."

All Due Respect

Chris Rhatigan posted "I cut my teeth in crime fiction with zines like *Pulp Metal*, *A Twist of Noir*, *Thuglit*, *Powder Burn Flash*, *Shotgun Honey*, and, of course, *All Due Respect*. **Alec Cizak** started *ADR* in 2010 and handed it over to me in 2012. In 2013, I moved *ADR* to an ebook/print format, then in 2014 expanded into book publishing, eventually shutting down the short fiction side of the venture.

An Astounding 90 Years of *Analog Science Fiction and Fact*

Statistician and author Michael F. Flynn served as Keynote Speaker at the 2019 City Tech Science Fiction Symposium.

All symposium photos by Ché Ryback.

Author and panel moderator Frank Wu.

Below left to right: Emily Hockaday, Trevor Quachri, and Stanley Schmidt.

An Astounding 90 Years of *Analog Science Fiction and Fact*

Analog kicked off the 90th year with a symposium co-coordinated by Professor **Jason Ellis** of City Tech College and managing editor **Emily Hockaday**. The event featured **Mike Flynn** as the keynote speaker, with an editorial panel of **Stanley Schmidt**, **Trevor Quachri**, and Emily Hockaday, and an author panel with *Analog* writers **Phoebe Barton, Leah Cypess,** **Jay Werkheiser, Frank Wu**, and **Alison Wilgus**. Academic papers were presented on gender representation in the magazine and field, humor in science fiction, the history of fact articles in *Analog*, and other fascinating topics. The entire symposium was captured on video and are embedded on the City Tech website: <https://openlab.citytech. cuny.edu/sciencefictionatcitytech>

Left: Author Louis Evans with Publisher Peter Kanter.

Below left to right: Author's panel with Alison Wilgus, Leah Cypess, Phoebe Barton, and Jay Werkheiser.

"All Due Respect <all-due-respect.blogspot.com> is returning in its original form, a zine that publishes one short story per month. The aesthetic will remain the same hard-as-nails crime fiction. About 1500–3000 words. **David Nemeth**, of Unlawful Acts <unlawfulacts.net> fame, and I will be co-editors. David does more for the crime fiction community than just about anyone and I'm thrilled to have him on board. All published stories will be collected into an annual anthology to be published via Down & Out Books."

Steve Darnall: Nostalgia Digest

"The Spring 2020 issue of *Nostalgia Digest* will feature a cover story about the 50th anniversary of *Those Were the Days*, the radio show that led to the creation of this publication. The Spring issue of *Nostalgia Digest* will also include our Necrology for 2019, articles about the Golden Age of radio and movies and additional information about a special event commemorating *Those Were the Days*' Golden Anniversary."

Those Were the Days' 50th

"On Saturday, May 2, 1970, Chicagoans heard the debut of *Those Were the Days*, a radio show dedicated to preserving the sounds of radio's 'Golden Age,' a time radio was a 'theater of the mind,' allowing listeners to use their imaginations as they heard the top actors, comedians, musicians and writers of the era.

"It's fifty years later and radio has changed a lot since then. One thing hasn't changed: *Those Were the Days* is still on the air, celebrating the Golden Age of Radio, every Saturday afternoon on WDCB. Such endur-

Nostalgia Digest Winter 2020

ance in the face of changing times calls for a celebration, and *Those Were the Days* is planning a big one—a special live broadcast that will air on WDCB from 1 to 5 pm on Saturday, May 2, 2020 . . . fifty years to the day since *Those Were the Days* signed on for the first time. This special broadcast will originate from Chicago's Irish American Heritage Center (4604 N. Knox Avenue) as a benefit for WDCB, the radio home of *Those Were the Days* since 2001.

"In addition to *Those Were the Days* founder **Chuck Schaden**, current host **Steve Darnall** and longtime announcer **Ken Alexander**, this special anniversary show will present live re-creations of classic moments from the Golden Age of Radio, featuring guests **Patty McCormack** (*The Bad Seed*, *The Sopranos*), **Tim Kazurinsky** (*Saturday Night Live*), **Rich Koz** (Svengoolie),

Nostalgia Digest's Autumn 2019 Variants

Steve Darnall explains, "We wanted to do something special for our 45th anniversary issue and when we had the idea for a Wizard of Oz cover story—and realized we had two marvelous photos that would make great covers—we decided to publish variant covers. After all, why should *Entertainment Weekly* get all the fun of multiple covers?

"In terms of distribution, we tried to send equal copies of each issue to each distributor and to our mailing service. (That is, equal sized boxes—I wasn't about to ask anyone to pack copies of both covers into a single box.) The individual stores and subscribers got what they got. Some readers were confused by seeing a different cover on the copy in their local store but that didn't happen too often. (We still have copies of both issues at <nostalgiadigest.com>.) It was good fun and a nice way to celebrate a big anniversary."

Scott Lowell (*Queer As Folk*), **Trace Beaulieu** and **Kevin Murphy** (both from the Peabody Award-winning *Mystery Science Theater 3000*). Musical guests will include **The Dooley Brothers** and the **West End Jazz Band**, with more special guests to be announced. Tickets for this special live event are available for $50.00 apiece and can be purchased at WDCB.org, with all proceeds going to benefit WDCB.

"*Those Were the Days* has always been about taking sounds from the past and giving them a new life, and that's our goal with this 50th anniversary show," says Darnall, host of *Those Were the Days* since 2009. "We're delighted for the chance to

Pulp Modern and *Switchblade* special Tech Noir editions. Covers by Ran Scott and Scotch Rutherford.

honor this milestone anniversary and we're especially thrilled for the chance to celebrate both our show's history and radio's history with some very talented people who share our affection for the Golden Age of entertainment."

Those Were the Days is heard every Saturday afternoon from 1 to 5 pm on WDCB 90.9/90.7 FM. For archived episodes, visit <nostalgiadigest.com>.

Alec Cizak: Pulp Modern

Scotch Rutherford and **Alec Cizak** teamed last fall on the special Tech Noir editions of *Switchblade* and *Pulp Modern*. "We're aiming for a June release date for *Pulp Modern* No. 5," said Alec. "If we can get the summer issue out earlier, great, but June is the target month.

"Uncle B. Publications will also be publishing books, beginning with a single-volume that collects all the Drifter Detective novellas in one place. The Drifter Detective was a character created by **David Cranmer** of *Beat to a Pulp*. The bulk of the books were written by **Garnett Elliott**. *BTAP* has licensed the material to Uncle B. and we're hoping to bring a new audience to these classic pulp-style adventures. We're hoping they will be available by February/early March. We're also working on a charity anthology of crime stories that take place in Indianapolis called *Naptown Noir*. All proceeds will go to the Indiana Literacy Association. We're hoping to have this one out by June. Finally, for more adult fare, we'll be publishing a collection of novellas by **Alec Cizak**, **Scotch Rutherford**, and **Lisa Douglass** called *L.A. Stories*. The stories take place around the grindhouse days of Hollywood Blvd. Not recommended

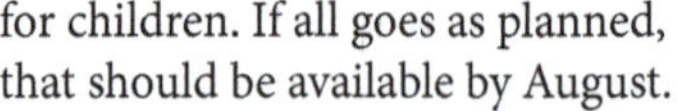

Asimov's Jan/Feb 2020

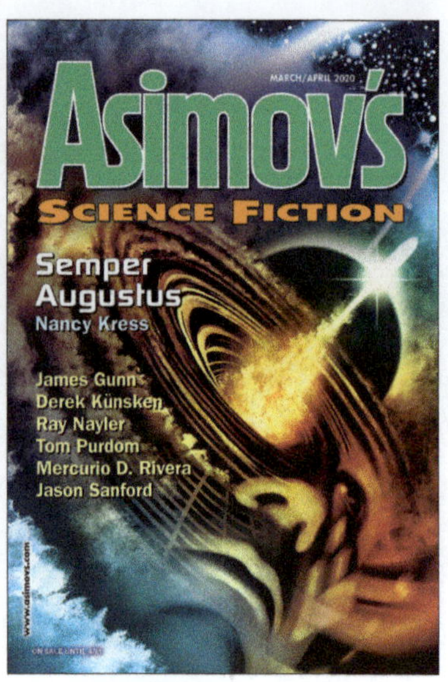

Asimov's Mar/Apr 2020

for children. If all goes as planned, that should be available by August.

"As for my writing, I'll be turning in the final book in the unofficial trilogy that began with *Down on the Street* and continued with *Breaking Glass*. We will learn the fate of Lester Banks, the protagonist of *Down on the Street*. That should be available from ABC Group Documentation by the middle of 2020."

Scotch Rutherford: Switchblade

After an impressive year with four issues of *Switchblade* regular, two special editions (*Stiletto Heeled* and *Tech Noir*), and guest editing *Pulp Modern: Tech Noir*, Scotch is ready to cut back to two issues of the "Anthology of Noir" in 2020. Writers take note: submissions will reopen in April 2020. And a new collaboration with **Alec Cizak** will begin.

Emily Hockaday: Asimov's

"Our May/June 2020 is stuffed with compelling novelettes! In 'Tun-

nels,' **Eleanor Arnason** escorts us to a distant future where her characters discover a complex web of dangerous intrigue. The world of **Ian R. MacLeod's** brilliant tale, 'The Mrs. Innocents,' which is both similar and very different from our own, hinges on one woman's powerful sacrifice. 'Ronni and Rod' face catastrophic disaster in **David Gerrold** & **Ctein's** new tale; **James Gunn's** 'Against the Stars' continues the pursuit of a mysterious A.I.; a young woman comes of age in **Tegan Moore's** 'Perfect Blue;' and in his first story for *Asimov's*, **Brad Aiken** teams with **Rick Wilber**, one of the magazine's veteran authors, for a trip to 'Ithaca.' **Ian Watson's** short story investigates the classic 'Brave New World by Oscar Wilde'; torn with guilt, **Bruce McAllister's** hero must listen to 'The Voice;' new to *Asimov's* author **Alice Towey** takes us to 'The River' to experience a young woman's excruciating adaptation to a brain implant; another new to *Asimov's* author **Evan Marcroft** visits the gods in 'Pax Mongolica;' and **Dominica Phetteplace** imagines a chilling future in 'Digital Witness.' You'll be 'Living in Wartime' in the issue's thrilling novella by **R. Garcia y Robertson**! We also anticipate a very special Guest Editorial by astronaut **Cady Coleman**.

"In future issues, we'll also be featuring tales from **Hollis Joel Henry**, **Robert Reed**, **M. Bennardo**, **Leah Cypess**, **Yue Pang**, **Rod Garcia** and **Gray Rinehart**."

Gary Lovisi: Gryphon Books

Paperback Parade No. 106 includes a look at the rare Australian Scientific Thriller series. Also coming in future issues are the UK Tit Bit crime and science fiction books, Spanish 1950s SF books, Tiki paperbacks, and of course much more.

Coming up on Gary's YouTube channel <youtube.com/channel/UCtTbibKhvzfDP-G7Ff-iJ_A> Gary says, "I will be looking at a lot of scarce series, Canadian, UK, Australian, and of course US vintage paperbacks." Gary has already produced and posted over 60 segments about rare and collectible books, as well as titles he has published like *Hardboiled* and *Paperback Parade*. He typically adds four to six new episodes a week! It's easy to subscribe to be sure you don't miss a topic.

Gary has also been writing. New stories and articles are coming to **Marvin Kaye's** *Sherlock Holmes Mystery Magazine* from Wildside, a novella for Airship27's *Holmes Consulting Detective* series, and a collection of Griff & Fats stories from Pulpventure Press called *Hardcases & Homicide*.

Broadswords and Blasters No. 12 Winter 2020. Cover by Luke Spooner.

Matthew Gomez, Cameron Mount: Broadswords and Blasters

"The truth is, we are going to put *Broadswords and Blasters* on indefinite hiatus after issue 12. We've had a good run, but both of us want to work on different projects, and well, we'd like to think we are ending on a high note.

"That said, we are releasing a double issue (18 writers), some who are veterans of our pages (**Richard Rubin**, **Steve DuBois**, **Matt Spencer**, **J. Rohr**, **DJ Tyrer**) as well as a few new faces."

Chuck Carter: Mystery Weekly Magazine

"We're sponsoring both the Best Crime Novella and Best Crime Short Story categories of Crime Writers of Canada <crimewriterscanada.com>. And as always, subscriptions to *MWM* are available on Kindle Newsstand with a 30 day free trial."

Mystery Weekly Magazine January 2020.
Cover by Robin Grenville-Evans.

The Paperback Fanatic No. 43 due out in
January 2020.

Justin Marriott:
Paperback Fanatic

"*The Paperback Fanatic* No. 43 will be out in January 2020—a Gold Medal special, with 88 full-colour pages devoted to the legendary publisher. It includes articles on authors **Gil Brewer**, **Dan Marlowe**, and **Charles Williams**; a visual guide to **Robert McGinnis**; and reviews of key Gold Medal titles.

"*Pulp Horror: All Review Special* will be out in Spring 2020. It features 120 reviews of horror paperbacks, pulps, magazines and comics from 1920 to 1989. Reviews include **H.P. Lovecraft**, **Robert Bloch**, **Graham Masterton**, **Jules De Grandin**, The Guardians, Skywald, Warren, *Weird Tales*, movie tie-ins, and much more.

"*Hot Lead: All Review Special* will be out in Summer 2020, with 150+ reviews of western paperbacks and comics. Reviews include **Louis L'Amour**, **George G. Gilman**, **Lewis Patten**, **Harry Whittington**, **Nelson Nye**, **Ralph Hayes**, **Don-**ald **Hamilton**, **T.V. Olsen**, **Luke Short**, **Louis Masterton**, and the inevitable, much, much more."

All of Justin's title are available through <amazon.com>.

Doug Draa: Weirdbook

As of mid-December the proofs on *Weirdbook* No. 42, the **All-John Shirley** issue, are expected any day. Corrections for the proofs for the first issue of the *Startling Stories* relaunch have gone back in production. The cover shown here is the proof—**Robert Silverberg's** name will be added to the production version.

Michael Bracken:
Black Cat Mystery Magazine

"*Black Cat Mystery Magazine* No. 5 was just released. Next up is a special edition: *Black Cat Mystery Magazine Presents Private Eyes*, an all-P.I. issue.

"The first season of *Guns + Tacos*, a serial novella anthology series that

Hot Lead: All Review Special with wraparound cover, due out in Summer 2020.

Trey R. Barker and I co-created and co-edit for Down & Out Books just ended in December. All six of the novellas will be collected into a pair of paperbacks scheduled for release in the first quarter of 2020. The first will contain my novella 'Three Brisket Tacos and a Sig Sauer,' and 'Plantanos con Lechera and a Snub-Nosed .38,' a special bonus story I wrote, which is only available to subscribers, will appear in the second. *Guns + Tacos* has been renewed for a second season and we're

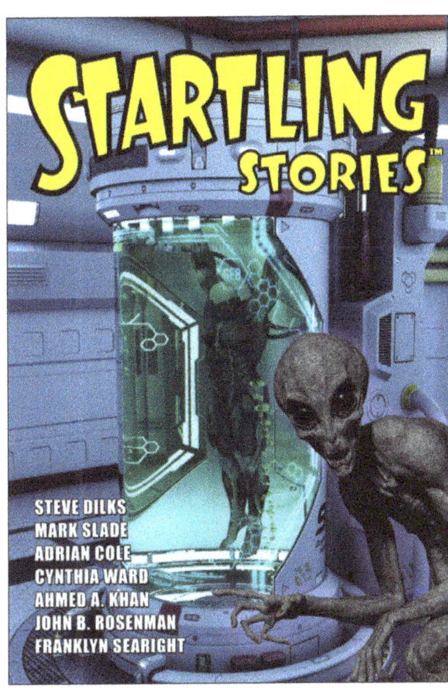

Startling Stories No. 1, first proof cover.

Black Cat Mystery Magazine No. 5

Down & Out: The Magazine Vol. 2 No. 1

Let's Play Make-Beleive, one of James O. Born's novels for James Patterson's digest-size Bookshots series.

working on prepping it for monthly release beginning in July 2020.

"I have two stories coming out in *Alfred Hitchcock's Mystery Magazine* sometime in 2020: 'Woodstock' and 'Sleepy River.' 'Where's Sara Jane,' co-authored with **Sandra Murphy** will appear in *Mid-Century Murder* (Darkhouse Books), and 'Goobers,' also co-authored with Sandra Murphy, will appear in *The Book of Impossible Crimes* (Mango Publishing). 'Of Memories Dying' will be reprinted in *Horror for the Throne* (Gray Rabbit Publications)."

Rick Ollerman: Down & Out: The Magazine

"The next issue of *The Magazine* with a feature story by **James O. Born**, an extremely entertaining speaker whose seminars and conference appearances are not to be missed. He's operated at seemingly every level of law enforcement and he's written books by

himself and lately he's become part of the **James Patterson** machine. There's also a story by **Don Stoll** in his "Ellen Flay" series, but that's all that's definite right now.

"Other than that, I can't say when any of the other things I'm working on will be available. Maybe an anthology of PBO authors from among those published by Stark House, which will also include a previously unpublished novel by **Jada Davis** (it would've made for a very solid Gold Medal back in the day). I'm still playing catch-up and although there are fewer things on the plate, it's still a full plate."

Art Taylor

This year's Bouchercon awarded Art a Macavity Award for his "English 398: Fiction Workshop" from *Ellery Queen's* Jul/Aug 2018. Bouchercon organizers signed Art to edit next year's anthology from Wildside Press that will include stories by conference guests of honor **Scott Turow**, **Walter Mosley**, **Anne Perry**, **Anthony Horowitz**, **Cara Black**, and **Catriona McPherson**—as well as a dozen or more stories chosen by Art through a blind submission process.

Art placed his first story for *Alfred Hitchcock* in the Jan/Feb 2020 issue, "The Boy Detective and The Summer of '74." The story will also be included in a collection of Art's stories from Crippen & Landru, set for release in February 2020.

Jennifer Landels: Pulp Literature

"Our big news at the moment is the Dec. 2019 release of the trade and ebook versions of **Matthew Hughes'** magnum opus, *What the Wind Brings*. It's a Spartacus story, set in the mysterious, deadly rainforests of 16th Century Ecuador. Against all odds, a reluctant young hero rises to lead fellow escaped slaves and indigenous tribes against the might of the Spanish throne to create a new country. Matthew Hughes' outstanding tale unites the beauty of The Mission with a stirring clash of swords, suspense, mysticism, and epic battle strategy.

"Another Dec. 2019 release: *Pulp Literature* No. 25: Step backstage with **AM Dellamonica**, enter the realms of myth with **Graham Robert Scott** and **Wallace Cleaves**, meet very different genies with **Akem** and **Susan Pieters**, and explore love, grief, guilt, and forgiveness with **Rebecca Ruth Gould**, **Allison Bannister** and **Frances Rowat**. All this plus a new **Frankie Ray** novella, an Irdaign story that prequels *Allaigna's Song*, poetry from **Matthew Walsh**, **David Troupes**, and **Nicholas Alti**, and the winners of the Hum-

mingbird Flash Fiction Prize.

"And this spring we're about to release *Allaigna's Song: Aria*, the sequel to *Overture*. *Allaigna's Song: Aria* picks up three days after *Overture* leaves off. Allaigna's ire

Pulp Literature No. 25 Winter 2020.

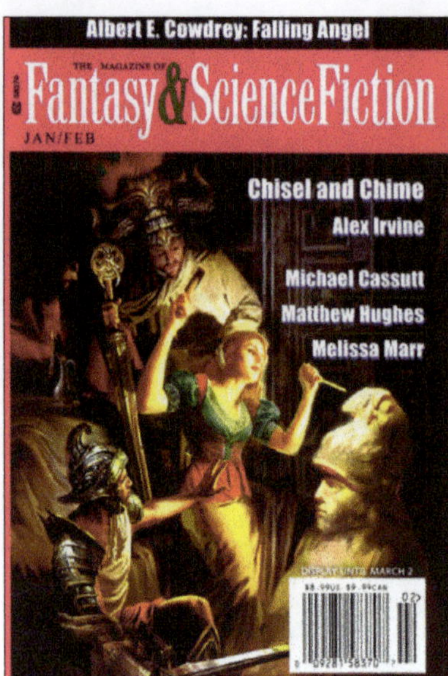

Publisher of *Fantasy & Science Fiction,*
Gordon Van Gelder, shared this cover of the
Jan/Feb 2020 issue.

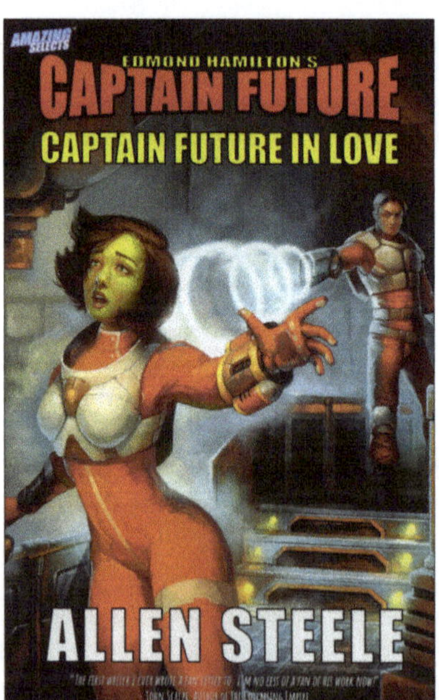

Experimenter Publishing launched a new
series in Fall 2019: *Amazing Selects. Captain
Future In Love* by Allen Steele is the first novel
in a series. The story was originally serialized in
the pages of the new *Amazing Stories.*

hasn't cooled, but the perils of the road provide more than a distraction. An encounter with a wild boar escalates to a run-in with poachers, leading to unlikely allies, subterfuge, captivity, and assault, which changes Allaigna's status from mere runaway to fugitive."

J.D. Graves: EconoClash Review

Brief, but no less substantial news from your friendly neighborhood Quality Cheap Thrills iconoclast: Down & Out books will become the publisher of *ECR* beginning with issue No. 5, coming early in 2020.

Tom Brinkmann

Sadly, an entry of Tom's well-researched articles on unusual off-the-beaten-path magazines is absent from our pages this issue due to events beyond his control. Hopefully, he'll return next issue. In the meantime, he's produced a stunning new edition of his mini artzine, *Squint* No. 7. For details, contact Tom at <vaioduct@aol.com>.

Marc Myers

Over the past few issues, Marc's striking collage work has become a staple of our pages. And this issue is no exception: see Marc's imagery for **Vince Nowell, Sr.'s** story "The Good Soldier" beginning on page 110. Marc's latest artzine is *Mulmig* No. 2. For details, contact him at <muckmires@hotmail.com>.

LOCs about TDE10

Tore Stokka: "About your monster coverboy: I may not be the first or the only one to mention this, but anyway: in 2011 **Greg Ketter** of Dreamhaven published

Squint No. 7 by Tom Brinkmann

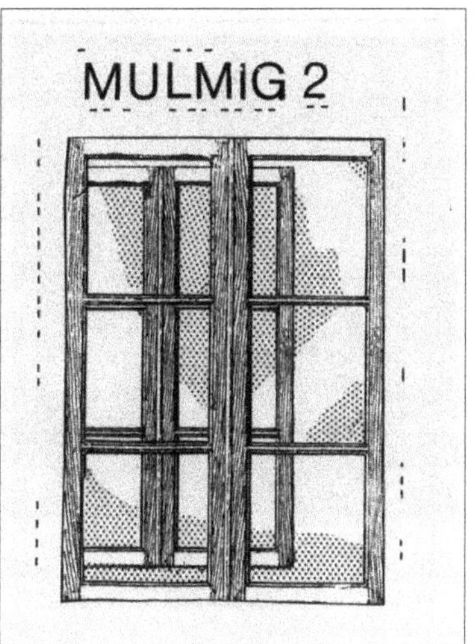

Mulmig No. 2 by Marc Myers

the first US edition of the **Vargo Statten** novelisation. It had an intro by **David Schow**, dozens of photos, some of which have never been published before. The book came in three states: trade paperback, hardcover and leather-bound hardcover. The latter was signed by **Ricou Browning** and **Julie Adams**." Tore also said he enjoyed the articles on Charlie Chan and **Sol Cohen**.

Tom Brinkmann's article on The Creature and **Marilyn Monroe** also sparked some memories that **Vince Nowell, Sr.** shared. "She was once a close part of our family in that as a young girl she and my late oldest (half-)brother Wally were playmates in a day-care arrangement. That's because Marilyn's (Norma Jean's) mother, **Gladys Baker**, and my mother worked together as film cutters (editors) in the early days of silent motion pictures. Gladys, another lady (young girl) named **Grace McKee**, and my mother were the so-called "Three Musketeers" at the various film studios of the day

in the early 1920s. Need I say that this was long before I was born.

"My mother married and had a child, Wally, in 1926. (Wally's father died in 1928.) Gladys had her illegitimate baby in 1927. When my mother married again, to my father in 1933, Gladys was one of the witnesses on the marriage license. I have photos of all of them on an automobile outing on or about that day. Norma Jean was a scrawny 6-year-old little blonde girl in the photos of her with Wally and with my father.

I never met Marilyn, I'm sad to say. But Wally and my mother kept in touch with her as she grew into adulthood and during her career as a model and later a starring actress. According to my mother, she was actually a sweet. shy young woman. My late brother told me she was always a bit "lost" amidst all the lights and glamour. I get the impression that she was never truly 'at home' with Hollywood and all that went with it."

Alfred Hitchcock's Mystery Magazine sports a new masthead for 2020.
Left: Jan/Feb, Right: Mar/Apr.

Jackie Sherbow:
Alfred Hitchcock & Ellery Queen

"With the May/June 2020 issues, *Ellery Queen's Mystery Magazine* and *Alfred Hitchcock's Mystery Magazine* will launch true crime features in the print magazines. Historian and true crime writer **Dean Jobb's** web-only column 'Stranger Than Fiction' will begin appearing in each issue of *EQMM*, with supplemental monthly columns on the web. 'Stranger Than Fiction' focuses on historical crimes, unique cases, and true crime book reviews. Author and former police officer **Lee Lofland** will be taking over *AHMM*'s 'Case Files' department with a column each issue. 'Case Files' will present topics around investigative and forensic procedures. *EQMM* and *AHMM* will also be joining forces for a true crime podcast, planned to launch in 2020.

"*AHMM*'s March/April 2020 issue, on sale Feb. 18 2020, will contain stories by **Jim Fusilli**, **Catherine Dilts**, and **Rachel Howzell Hall**. The May/June issue, on sale April 21, 2020, will feature a Mystery Classic by **Joyce Porter**, introduced by **Russell Atwood**. The 2020 Black Orchid Novella Award winner will be included in the July/August 2020 issue, on sale June 16, 2020.

"*EQMM*'s March/April 2020 issue, on sale Feb. 18 2020, features a novella by **Joyce Carol Oates**. The 2019 *EQMM* Readers Award winners and runners up will be announced in the May/June 2020 issue, on sale April 21, 2020. In the spring, you'll also see stories from **Keith McCarthy**, **David Dean**, and **Marilyn Todd**."

See page 149 for *EQMM* and *AHMM* at the Expo and Banquet.

Ellery Queen Mystery Magazine Left: Jan/Feb 2020, Right: Mar/Apr. 2020.

Acknowledgments
Many thanks to *TDE*'s readers and contributors for your support. Many of the enthusiasts who helped spread the word about *TDE10* are listed below. All comments and ratings are greatly appreciated. My apologies if I've left anyone out.

Advertising
Mystery Weekly Magazine
<mysteryweekly.com>
Pulp Literature <pulpliterature.com>
Pulp Modern
<pulp-modern.blogspot.com>
Switchblade <switchblademag.com>

Blog Posts/Newsletters
Pulp Literature <pulpliterature.com>
James Reasoner
<jamesreasoner.blogspot.com>
Stark House Press <starkhousepress.com>
Bill Thom <PulpComingAttractions.com>
Kevin Tipple <shortmystery.blogspot.com>

Ratings/Reviews/Listings
(Amazon, Goodreads)
Gazmend Kryeziu, Geographer, halfdan, Karl, Kim, Lee, Mary, Michael Neno, Mike Lazur, Stacy, and Steve Alcorn.

Booksellers
Bud's Art Books
Mike Chomko Books

Social Media Posts, Shares, and Likes
(Facebook, etc.)
Jamie Lee Anderson, Graham Andrews, Thirsty Author, Leslie Berry, Donald J. Bingle, Michael Bracken, David Brinkmann, Mary Burgess, CF Carter, Melissa Carter, Alec Cizak, Steve Cooper, Carla Kaessinger Coupe, Steve Davidson, Clark Dissmeyer, Ricko Drofdarb, Peter Enfantino, Jonathan Falk, Danny Ferbert, Brad W. Foster, Tim Fuller, Barb Goffman, JD Graves, Bruce Harris, John Hull, David Hyman, Rachel Krauss, Robert Lopresti, Jim Main, Paul D. Marks, Justin Marriott, Todd Mason, Rick McCollum, John O'Neill, Michael Neno, Mary Neno, Kathleen Banks Nutter, Jacques Nyemb, Aley Odagled, Josh Pachter, Dennis Palumbo, Brian Payne, Dee Dee Ploog, Lori-Ann Reif, Pilar Williams Seacord, Jim Shaffer, Kip Poe Speicher, Art Taylor, John Timm, Kevin Tipple, Marilyn Todd, Albert Tucher, Joseph Tura, Temple Walker, Edd Vick, Bob Vojtko, and Adam Yeater.

MADAME SELINA

Janice Law's portrait of Madame Selina and Nip Tompkins

Janice Law

Interviewed by Richard Krauss

Janice Law is a retired college English teacher, painter, and author of mystery novels, historical novels, short stories, and as Janice Law Trecker, academic articles and history books. This interview was conducted via email in July 2019.

TDE: What sparked your interest in writing the Madam Selina series for *Alfred Hitchcock's Mystery Magazine*?

Janice Law: One day just heard Nip in my ear, but my advanced degrees are in English and American Lit, focus on the 19th century, and I have written books on the early feminist movement and 19th century history so I had a lot of background. That was the great era for spiritualism and mediums and Victoria Woodhull, pioneer feminist and early candidate for president, was a medium whose contact was the Greek orator Demosthenes.

TDE: What prompted the time and place of the series?

JL: I had a lot of background in the era and I had been interested in mediums as they were an important part of the period, especially in the post-Civil war era. But I never

Madam Selina, medium

Marcus Aurelius, spiritual guide

The leading cast members of the Madame Selina series, depicted by Alfred Klosterman.

intended the stories to be a series. In fact, when my then <Sleuthsayers.org> colleague Rob Lopresti suggested I do some more, I thought the idea was silly. However, the thought had been planted. . . .

TDE: The first story, appropriately called "Madame Selina," opens with the medium's selection of Nip Tompkins from the Orphan Home. How did you arrive at your decision for a young assistant, and for him to become narrator?

JL: He just showed up and I think any story with super-

natural aspects benefits from an at least partially skeptical narrator and observer.

TDE: The reporter, Jim Kaynes, also appears in the first adventure. Did you know from the start he'd be a recurring character?

JL: Not at all. He is a tribute to the clever but hard drinking old sports reporters who taught my husband the sports writing business in the late '50s and early '60s. Also, it soon became clear to me that Madame Selina would need sources. As she puts it, it was unrealistic to expect Aurelius to understand things like railroad stocks.

TDE: Despite the challenges of working for a medium, Nip makes it clear he's much happier with Madame Selina than at the orphanage, but in the second story "A Political Issue," she asks him to go undercover and "then I was once again the inmate of an orphanage." Why did you send him back?

JL: Well, when I started to

Nip Tompkins, cub reporter

Jim Kaynes, newsman

do more of the stories, I decided I would work through all the big topics of the period and also touch on some of the popular 19th century plots. The vulnerable orphan, endangered heiresses, and corrupt politicos were high on the list and only Nip could do the inside work at the orphanage.

TDE: The Madame's household is well funded, but in the next story, her livelihood is under threat from "The Psychic Investigator." What triggered your idea for this story?

JL: Spiritualism and mediums were both controversial and there were people attempting to debunk those who claimed access to the spirit world. A little later there were people (including Arthur Conan Doyle) who hoped to prove that spirits existed, so there was a lot of historical material to call on.

TDE: In "The Irish Boy" Maddie O'Rourke enlists the aid of Madame Selina and Nip to find her brother, Brian, who's gone missing. Besides solving the mystery, there's a nice bit at the end where Selina uses her influence to change the lad's bent. Are these ending "extras" something you add late in the writing process, or are they more central to where you're taking readers from the start?

JL: I'm afraid that almost nothing is planned from the start with me. Even when I was writing mystery novels (ie the Anna Peters and Francis Bacon series) I was lucky if I knew the victim and the perpetrator at the start. Usually I had a vague idea for a story or sometimes just an opening line. Literally!

TDE: In the series' fifth story, "The Ghostly Fireman," Nip tells us: "I reckon that Madam Selina, like most of us, is a mix of truth and imagination, and that Aurelius, who, as she often reminds me, pays the bills, sits on the border between real and not real. Every time I decide to put him firmly on one side or the other, he surprises me . . ." Why the ambivalence?

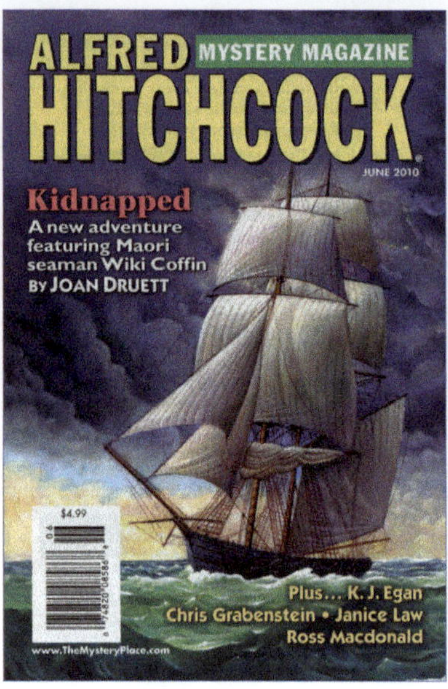

AHMM June 2010

AHMM Sept. 2013

JL: Well, Nip has a logical and rational mind, as I think you'll agree, yet Madame Selina is so convincing and so sincere and so clever in her own way that he is swayed toward Aurelius's reality on occasion. It is a token of the power of the imagination, which is Madame's real gift, that a boy like Nip gives him a certain reality.

TDE: The specter of charlatans emerges between a young woman and her brother over the fortunes of their deceased mother in "The Spiritualist," an adventure that takes Selina and Nip to Newport. What inspired this story?

JL: Again, I think the fact that mediums etc. were controversial and of course disputed wills, inheritance etc. is one of the great Victorian literary themes. We don't live that far from Newport and it was one of the great Gilded Age resorts.

TDE: The seventh story, "The Or-

gan Grinder's Daughter," foreshadows potential changes in the series, when Selina and Nip rescue Gabriella (the organ grinder's daughter) from a crime syndicate. By the end, Nip believes Madame Salina with train Gabriella as her apprentice, leaving his own role with some level of uncertainty. Changes are in store for Nip, but Gabriella is absent in the next outing. Will she return?

JL: I thought she might and envisioned a trip back to Italy with Madame S for her musical education but now I am not sure. I felt I had written as much as I could about the characters and wanted to move to something new. It is easy to get lazy with characters one enjoys and who write easily.

TDE: In the most recent story, "A Fine Nest of Rascals," Nip takes a job with a newspaper, working for Jim Kaynes, and Madame Salina reveals, ". . . I am think-

AHMM Dec. 2013

AHMM Jan/Feb 2015

ing of ending my career after my next engagement." Tell us more!

JL: "Rascals" was originally an entry in the Nero Wolfe Black Orchid competition. That's why it is longer. It was also my farewell to Madame Selina. If I do more in that period, I think I would concentrate on Nip, now almost entirely grown up and moving into a different era. The great spiritual crisis post Civil War was winding down, the country was focused on making money. At one of the "yellow journalism" newspapers, Nip would be in a good position for adventures. And Madame Selina, who was sincere in her beliefs, however much assistance she gave to Aurelius, was not one to make seances the entertainment for the rich and idle.

TDE: Fortune often shines on the series through interior illustrations, by such wonderful artists as Edward Kinsella III, Robyn Hyzy, Tim Foley,

Ally Hodges, and your "Rascals" cover art by Maggie Ivy. Do you often know about the artwork in advance? I believe the Madame herself is only shown in her first story and her cover story. You don't describe her appearance in detail—how close are these interpretations to your own vision of the character?

The Center of Spiritualism

In 1879, the Cassadaga Lake Free Association was incorporated as a meeting place for Spiritualists and Freethinkers. It became The City of Light in 1903, and finally the Lily Dale Assembly in 1906. The group's purpose is to further the science, philosophy, and religion of Spiritualism. Lily Dale became the center of the Spiritualist movement in the 19th Century and remains the world's largest facility of its kind, located on the shores of the Cassadaga Lakes, between Buffalo, NY and Erie, PA, and today offers a year-round schedule of lectures and workshops.

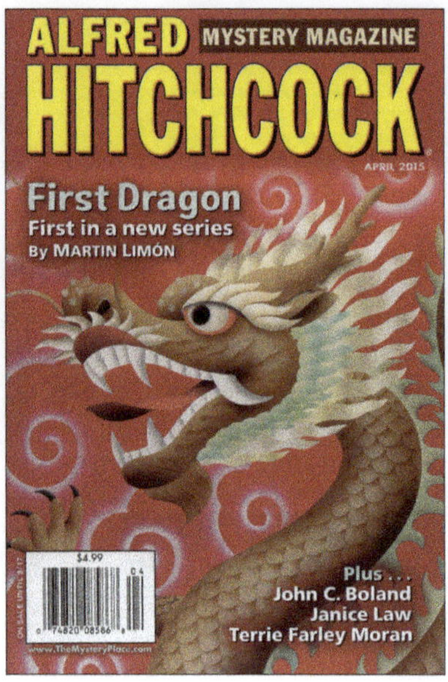

AHMM April 2015

AHMM March 2016

AHMM Jul/Aug 2016

JL: No, the artwork is always a surprise and I am always delighted to get an illustration of any kind. That said, my Madame Selina would look much more like a 40ish Victori-an woman of comfortable means. If I can find an illustration I did for my own pleasure, I will attach [page 20].

TDE: What's next for Madame Selina and friends?

JL: Unknown at this point.

TDE: Besides the Madam Selina series, what else have you written?

JL: I mentioned the Anna Peters series, (Edgar nominated, Houghton Mifflin, St. Martins) and the Francis Bacon series (Mysterious Press) (Lambda winner). I have written a number of standalone contemporary novels, *The Night Bus*, *The Lost Diaries of Iris Weed*, *Voices* and *Homeward Dove* (Wildside). The latter is available from Wildside, along with *Blood in the Water*, a collection of non-Madame S stories.

I have also published history books, scholarly articles and journalism.

TDE: How can readers keep up with your work?

JL: I regularly publish in

AHMM Jul/Aug 2019

AHMM, EQMM, Sherlock and *Black Cat.*

For more information about Janice and her work, visit her website, <janicelaw.com>, and <sleuthsayers.org> where she occasionally blogs.

Alfred Klosterman is a long time digest enthusiast. His illustrations have appeared inside and on the covers of dozens of publications including *Cemetery Dance, Thrust, Fantasy Tales,* and *Pulp Modern.* His portraits of the cast of the Madame Selina series marks his work's first appearance in *The Digest Enthusiast.*

PHANTOM BOOKS
An Original Mystery—Not A Reprint
Homicide Hotel
By Joe Barry
No. 500
35c
A Jealous Woman Plus a Faithless Lover Equals Murder!

Homicide Hotel

Review by Gary Lovisi

"I was halfway out the window when a hand like an ape's grabbed me by the hair and jerked me back into the room. The hand swung me by the hair into the arms of the other man. His right hand chopped down on my neck and I went limp."

This is an early paperback-related article I wrote that originally appeared in Jon White's *Paperback Forum* No. 2, way back in 1985, which was one of the pioneer precursors to my own magazine *Paperback Parade*. I updated and expanded it a bit for this special appearance in *The Digest Enthusiast*.

Yes, I admit it; I read it. Every word! From the sleazy exploitation bondage and torture cover, right on down to the very end of the story. Let me tell you it was quite an experience and a bit unexpected. It's one of those things every vintage paperback collector can't help to do at times—and therein lies a tale.

It all began during one of the long ago Sunday book shows that

Paperback Forum No. 2

Paperback Parade No. 53

were held at the New York Statler Hilton. I was looking through some nice old books when I was attracted by a loud *"Pssst!"* A disreputable character intent upon separating me from my money? Perhaps? Well, let us investigate. Slung over his shoulder was a large green army bag, which he opened with a provocative tease, whispering in a conspiratorial tone, *"You interested in any of these?"*

The bag was filled with vintage paperback goodies. Well, that did it, and I went to it like a fish to bait. With deft fingers, I looked through the lot (the loot!) and picked out a few cool items. Then he told me, *"Got something real special here."*

That's when he pulled out one of the 'holy grails' of crime digest paperbacks, *Homicide Hotel*. Well, I couldn't have been more surprised if he had produced *Zip Gun Angels*—but that's another story.

I knew this book was for me.

Homicide Hotel is a first edition (it has never been reprinted and likely never will be) published in 1951 by Phantom Books (No. 500, the first book in this short US run), by Joe Barry. Joe Barry was actually Barry Lake (for more on him see my article "The Elusive Joe Barry" in *Paperback Parade* No. 53). The book has what I would say is the most brutal torture/bondage cover art I have ever seen on a vintage era digest. It shows a young and beautiful woman made up with hot red lipstick, tied to a chair, menaced by two nasty thugs. One holds a bottle of chloroform, while the other brutally pulls her head up by the hair! The terror is clearly seen in her face and eyes as the men advance to do their worst. Talk about violence towards women! This cover really takes the case. It is quite disgusting in those terms. The fact that anyone, anywhere, would issue a book with so offensive a cover—even by old-time paperback publishers who were notorious for doing anything to make a sale—strained my credulity about the value of the writing and story between the covers. I had to find out. Well, the price was right, so I took it home and looked it over. The more I looked, the more intrigued I became, until I took the plunge and I knew I had to read *Homicide Hotel*.

It is not what I thought at all.

Basically, the book is a murder mystery novel with a hard-boiled detective a la Raymond Chandler's Philip Marlowe, or Dashiell Hammett's Sam Spade, who tracks down the girlfriend of a rubbed out mobster whose stash of millions of dollars also disappeared when the girl did. Detective Donn O'Mara

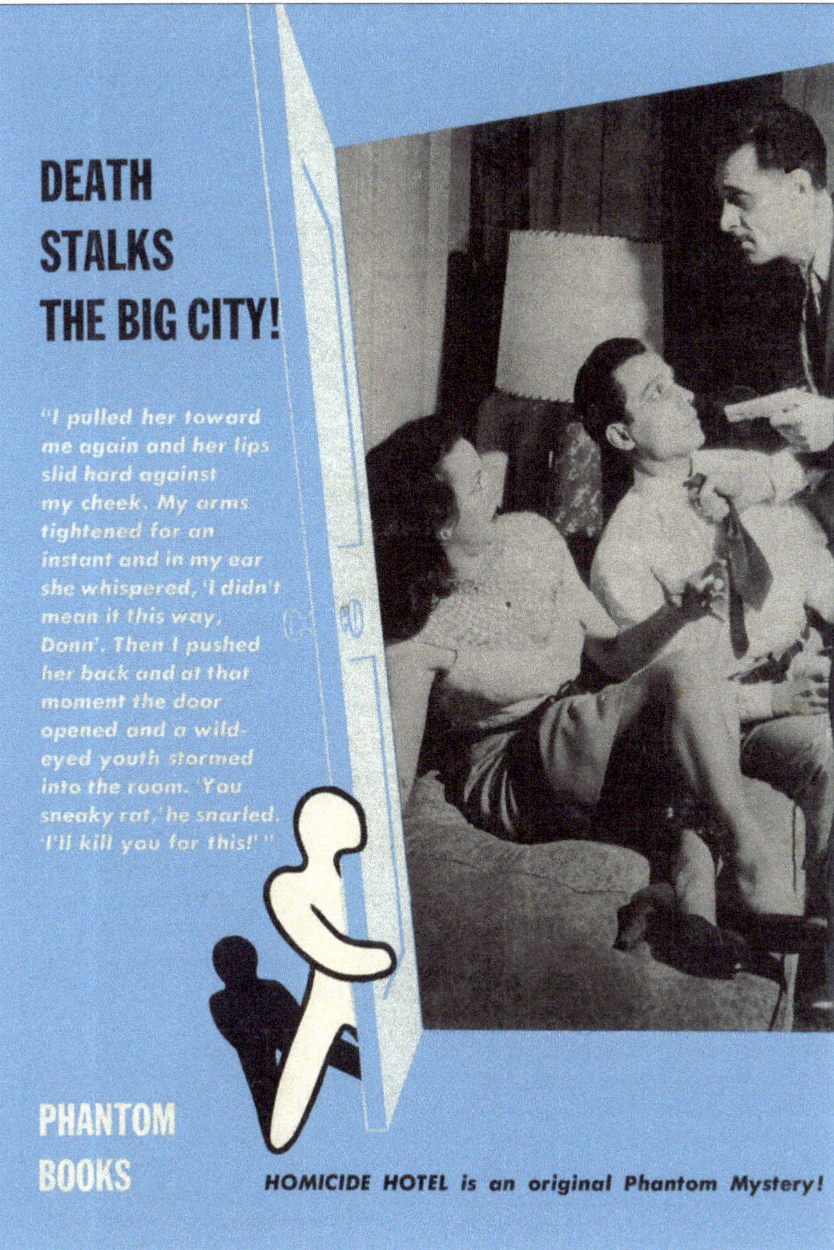

Homicide Hotel Phantom Books No. 500 back cover

is just as hard-boiled as Spade and Marlowe, and while he is as tough as Mickey Spillane's Mike Hammer, he is nowhere as brutal and perhaps a bit smarter. O'Mara is actually thoughtful and intelligent, and the story is a tightly plotted novel of interesting characters whose motives kept me guessing until the very end.

And you know what? Surprise! It's a damn good book!

Of course, the package is something else altogether. Friends who saw me reading it at work were wondering just what kind of weird stuff I was getting into. Not to worry I told them, just research for an article on old paperback books I was writing. Sure, they replied, and they looked at me a bit funny.

Aside from O'Mara finding the body of a murdered man in a hotel (and this takes up about one page of the book) the story doesn't even take place in a hotel at all! Then why the title? And as for that example of unbelievably brutal bondage/torture art on the cover—no scene or event even remotely close to this occurs in the book at all. The cover doesn't even excerpt a minor scene from the novel and expand upon it, which many paperback publishers used to do in their cover art, to exploit a sale. Back then they would have the artist illustrate only the most 'juicy part.' Of course there is some violence in this novel—this is, after all, a murder mystery—but there are very few killings and all of them take place off stage. There is no lingering on violence, such as in modern slasher movies. No sadism here in the story at all. Except for that cover art!

Aside from O'Mara getting beaten up and punching a gangster, and a gangster's moll, he is a remarkably good and well-behaved fellow. In fact, he meets a nice girl, falls in love, and though tempted by at least two other women, stays loyal to his gal. In the end, he finds love and happiness with her in a truly happy ending.

But this is still a tough, hard crime novel that fans of the genre will want to read, and they will enjoy it. Unfortunately, I do not know who the artist was who did the cover art. The book is just one of 14 in the US Phantom Books digest series of crime novels published in 1951 to 1952. It is a key digest series, with some important and expensive books among those 14 titles, including original digest-size novels by Day Keene and Harry Whittington. The books are numbered from No. 500 to 513, with *Homicide Hotel* being the first book in the series. Phantom Books would also become a series of digest crime pulp novels published in Australia with redrawn covers from the American paperback editions—and that Aussie series would run to over 300 books!

However, it all began with *Homicide Hotel* and Joe Barry, who has written a book full of action and suspense that keeps you reading. It is a classic crime novel noir not to be missed by any fan of the genre. Hard to believe it when you look at that cover.

But, then, you know what they say about judging a book by the cover . . . .

Gary Lovisi is an author, bookseller, and collector who writes about collectable paperbacks. Under his Gryphon Books imprint, he publishes *Paperback Parade*, the world's leading magazine on collectable paperbacks of all kinds. You can find out more about Gary and his work at his website: <gryphonbooks.com>.

Stark House Press

ORRIE HITT
WRITING AS KAY ADDAMS
Warped Desire /
The Strangest Sin
978-1-944520-95-3 $19.95
Two of Hitt's lesbian novels from the
early 1960s, with an exciting, new
introduction by James Reasoner, who
calls these books "a potent combination,
a one-two punch of solid storytelling and
characterization and heart."
November 2019.

LIONEL WHITE
Coffin for a Hood /
Operation—Murder
978-1-944520-83-0 $19.95
Two 1950s thrillers from the author
whom the New York Times called the
"master of the big caper."
"Smart, fast, hard-edged storytelling."
—Don Crinklaw, *Booklist*.
New introduction by Ben Boulden.
November 2019.

STARK HOUSE PRESS
1315 H Street, Eureka, CA 95501
707-498-3135 www.StarkHousePress.com
Available from your local bookstore, or direct from the publisher.

Manhunt 1954 part three

Synopses by Peter Enfantino

"We worked the clock around, four of us at a time, in three shifts, so that it was two to one it wouldn't happen on my tour."

"A Life for a Life" by Robert Turner *Manhunt* December 1954

Vol. 2 No. 9 November 1954
144 pages, 35 cents

Pistol by Hal Ellson, illo: Lee (4000 words) ★★★

To impress his fellow gang members, Dusty must come up with a gun to rumble with. Written much like a diary, "Pistol" is an impressive debut for Hal Ellson, who would contribute a total of 23 stories throughout the run of *Manhunt*. According to Ellson's bio, his stories are "based on his experience with these teen-age gangs and have gained the praise of critics and readers not only for their excitement and realistic pace and tone, but for their obvious authenticity." Ellson's other contributions to gang-related fiction included his million-seller *Duke*, about a gang of Harlem youths.

Replacement by Jack Ritchie, illo: Tom O'Sullivan (3000 words) ★★

Max Warren wants to move

Manhunt Vol. 2 No. 9 November 1954

up fast in the chain of command in the local organization. Once he gets there, he decides he wants all that goes with the job, including the boss' woman. Interesting story marred by a bad last line.

Shy Guy by Robert Turner, illo: Lee (3000 words) ★★★

Della, now employed and feeling free, tries to push her husband Artie into her newfound world of alcohol and business parties. When

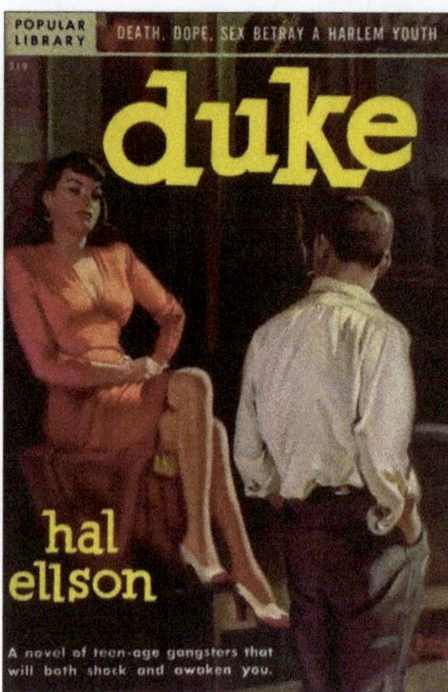

Duke by Hal Ellson (Popular 219, 1950).
Cover by Rudolph Belarski.

the parties turn to wife-swapping, Artie's had enough and cracks under the strain. Years before this fiction became famous in the hands of Jacqueline Susann and her ilk, "Shy Guy" was a daring little story. It's lost a lot of its punch, of course, but it's still fairly effective.

Man from Yesterday

by Jonathan Craig, illo: Ray Houlihan (5000 words) ★★★

Detectives Lew Keller and Burt Ogden must solve the intriguing case of a man found in a car murdered. Their trail leads to a married woman the man had been seeing. Though "Man From Yesterday" can be very dry at times (Craig has that *Dragnet*-style dialog down pat), I still found it an enjoyable read. Halfway through the story, Ed Seibert, a PI makes a brief appearance. This reminded

me of the crossovers that populated such seventies shows as *Cannon* and *Barnaby Jones*. A nice touch and Seibert seems to be a character that Craig should have spun off.

A Bull to Kill by Richard Marsten, illo: Tom O'Sullivan (4000 words) ★★★

Reardon, a rare American bullfighter has had everything taken away from him: his beloved Juanita, lost to fellow toreador Gomez; his nerve, to a recent goring; and the crowd that once cheered his name and now favors the upstart Gomez. Driven to madness, Reardon decides he will fight one more bull and then kill Gomez. Marsden (McBain) again proves he can't be pigeonholed. "A Bull to Kill" is as far removed from an 87th Precinct mystery as you can get.

The Stalkers by Grant Colby, illo: Lee (1000 words) ★

Ben is released from the sanitarium and presumed sane. He acts sane until he imagines his parakeet and puppy are stalking him.

The Wet Brain by David Alexander, illo: Ray Houlihan (7500 words) ★½

A "wet brain" is a derogatory term for an alcoholic so far gone that he loses all sense of reality and place. This particular "wet brain" is convinced he's killed someone but can't convince anyone else. He's wandering the Bowery with a pocket full of money and attracting the attention of fellow booze hounds.

David Alexander, according to his *Manhunt* bio, "insures the accuracy of his stories through study of actual police procedure, and graduated at the head of a recent class in Criminology given by a former New

York police inspector. Alexander was the author of several crime novels, among them: *Murder Points a Finger* (1953), *Murder in Black and White* (1951), *Paint the Town Black* (1956), *Die, Little Goose* (1956) and the b-side of Robert Bloch's *Spider-web* (Ace Double, 1954), *The Corpse in My Bed* (a retitling of his first novel, *Most Men Don't Kill*, 1951).

The Man Who Had Too Much to Lose by Hampton Stone, illo: Ray Houlihan (23,500 words) ★★½

Assistant District Attorney Jeremiah X. Gibson happens to be in the right place at the right time when he witnesses portly Jason Gracie fall ill from what appears to be poisoning. Gracie, a belligerent and pompous individual, refuses to believe this theory until his chef is found dead, poisoned. It's up to Jeremiah to sort through the motives and alibis of the cast of characters that surround Jason Gracie. Very much in the Perry Mason tradition, "The Man Who Had Too Much to Lose" is not a bad read, despite its length and its "cozy" atmosphere, which I usually find detrimental to a story published in *Manhunt*.

Published in hardcover by Simon and Schuster in 1955 and reprinted by Dell in paperback in 1957. Eighteen novels featuring DA Jeremiah X. "Gibby" Gibson and his helper, Mac, were published between 1948 and 1972. More interesting is the reprinting that took place in 1972 as part of the "Hampton Stone Mystery" series of paperbacks published by Paperback Library. Seventeen of the novels were reprinted in the series ("The Man Who Had Too Much to Lose" was No. 16). Strangely enough, the

Ed McBain's Mystery Book No. 3 1961. Cover by Harry Bennett.

18th, published in 1972, was never reprinted in paperback (in the series or otherwise). Hampton Stone was the pseudonym of prolific author Aaron Marc Stein (1906–1985), who wrote over a hundred novels under his own name, as Stone, and also as George Bagby. "The Man Who Had Too Much to Lose" would be Gibby Gibson's only appearance in *Manhunt* but Gibson would later pop up in "The Mourners at the Bedside", a short story in *Ed McBain's Mystery Book* No. 3 (1961).

Vol. 2 No. 10 December 1954
144 pages, 35 cents

Pretty Boy by Hal Ellson, illo: Tom O'Sullivan (3000 words) ★

From what I could make out between all the hip jive-talk, this is about a young man caught up in the gang life. I'd have preferred

Manhunt Vol. 2 No. 10 December 1954

to read the translated text.

That night I bought me some reefers. I got crazy high quick and sent Zelda home for my pistol. Then I picked up the rest of the boys, cause we got a "war" on with the Pelicans. We taxied into foreign territory, fired a few wild shots and flew, cause the cops was hot in the streets.

Ellson's bio in "Mugged and Printed" touts this as "another tough and realistic picture of teen gang life."

Two Little Hands by Fletcher Flora, illo: Houlihan (2000 words) ★★

Big, brawny Obie's not right in the head and everyone around him takes advantage of him, including our narrator, Jake. What Jake convinces Obie to do will haunt both of them the rest of their lives.

The Red Tears by Jonathan Craig, illo: James Sentz (5000 words) ★½

Detectives Fred Spence and Jake Thomas of the 18th Precinct catch the murder of a pretty girl, shot and robbed of her engagement ring, the titular "red tears." Not much more than a novel outline, "The Red Tears" goes from Point A to Point B very quickly and without much substance.

To a Wax Doll by Arnold Marmor (1000 words) ★★★

Very good short-short about a cop tracking down a heroin pusher. Last little bit adds a nice, nasty bite.

A Bachelor in the Making by Charles Jackson, illo: Tom O'Sullivan (2000 words) ★★

Yet another of the "slice of life" stories offered up by respectable authors outside the crime genre and ballyhooed in *Manhunt*. This one concerns a boy growing up and experiencing life while working in a grocery store. He doesn't witness a murder. He doesn't commit a murder. He just works and observes.

A Life for a Life by Robert Turner, illo: James Sentz (2500 words) ★★★

Three cops stake out a maternity ward, awaiting an escaped convict whose wife is giving birth. One of the cops is a trigger-happy sadist, who shows the con how good he is with a gun. Grisly climax when the con shows the cop how sadistic he can be.

Twilight by Hal Harwood (1000 words) ★★★

A man remembers a violent incident in his childhood. Brief, but powerful.

For a Friend by Bob McKnight, illo: Dick Shelton (1000 words) ★★★

Joe Rossotti's not a bright guy, but he has to have Carmen, a high-priced neighborhood "lady." Carmen suggests that if Joe had a grand, he'd get a grand time. She recommends the horses and even picks a horse for Joe to bet on. Since Joe's not that bright, he takes a while to realize he's been played. Unfortunately for Joe, his epiphany doesn't occur until after the race. But Joe concocts his revenge pretty quickly thereafter. Sly fun.

The Hero by Floyd Mahannah (5500 words) ★★

Mel Karger, just out of the pen, wants only a fresh start. Unfortunately, that fresh start may mean dealing with the rat who framed him.

Diary of a Devout Man by Max Franklin, illo: Dick Francis (3000 words) ★★★

Our titular character suddenly begins receiving messages from God telling him he has to wipe the world clean of sinners. He buys a gun and the first sinner to fall is his girlfriend. Max Franklin is a pseudonym for Richard Deming.

Oppurtunity by Russell E. Bruce, illo: Gussman (500 words) ★★

A newspaper reporter comes across evidence he can use to

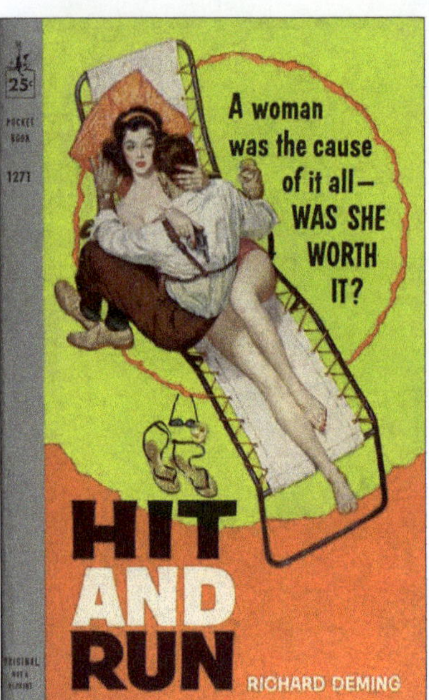

Hit and Run by Richard Deming
(Pocket Book 1271, 1960)

blackmail a mobster. Proof that not all short-shorts are bad.

The Housemother Cometh

by Hayden Howard, illo: Tom O'Sullivan (1500 words) ★

Beau and Fred sneak a woman into their dorm. A rare (and unwanted) excursion into comedy for *Manhunt*.

Manslaughter by Henry Ewald,

illo: James Sentz (1000 words) ★★

John Madden has lost his job and is facing tough times. When he goes to see his ex-boss, some hope arises. When that hope is dashed, he hits the bar and winds up in trouble.

Hit and Run by Richard Deming,

illo: Houlihan (16,000 words) ★★★★

Barney Calhoun steps out of the Happy Hollow Bar one night and witnesses a hit and run. Being a PI in a small town doesn't bring in a lot of dough, so Barney gets it into his head he'll act as middleman for the evil deed doers. He goes to Helena Powers, the passenger in the car, and offers a deal: he'll go to the victim (who's in intensive care) and offer to pay for his silence for a fee. Helena agrees, but unfortunately, things get complicated for Barney when the victim dies. A whole new plan comes into effect, including another murder, Helena's frightened lover, and an elaborate scheme to keep Helena and Barney out of jail. Deming crafts a wonderful short novel, filled with blind curves and capped off by a riotous climax. Later expanded to novel size (Pocket Book, 1960).

No Half Cure by Robert E. Murray,

illo: Gussman (1000 words) ★

Doctor Kleist is helping socialite Mrs. Clinton overcome her annoying and embarrassing habit of kleptomania. Of course, he cures her but it's revealed that the doctor himself is a kleptomaniac and has stolen Mrs. Clinton's expensive cigarette case. A one-note joke extended to 1000 words.

Judgment by G. H. Williams,

illo: Coughlin (1000 words) ★★★

In an issue filled with too many short-shorts, there are a surprising number of bright lights. This is one of them. Two punks are giving a bartender a hard time. They don't know he's got an itchy trigger finger.

Vol. 2 No. 11 Dec. 25th, 1954

144 pages, 35 cents

Crime of Passion

by Richard S. Prather,

illo: Dick Sheldon (3500 words) ★★

Shell Scott goes to a beach party where the host's later found on a spit, cooking like a pig. Unpleasant off day for Shell.

The Purple Collar

by Jonathan Craig, illo: Tom O'Sullivan (6000 words) ★

An 18th Precinct short mystery starring Pete Selby and his partner, Ben Muller. This time, the boys must solve the riddle of a hanged man who didn't die by hanging. Various characters are introduced, but the story never seems to be populated by real people. Again, this just reads like a knockoff of *Dragnet*, and though the 18th Precinct stories and the 87th Precinct tales of Ed McBain ran concurrently, the Craig stories come off as nothing more than weak imitations.

Flowers to the Fair by Craig Rice,

illo: Houlihan (6000 words) ★★

John J. Malone's latest client is a mousy accountant who's been embezzling money from his boss. The boss offers to loan the mouse enough money to pay him back and the next day the accountant is found dead. Smelling something fishy, John J. investigates the killing. Not a very entertaining read. John J. seems to be able to take many of his cases on for little or no money (because the client is a sympathetic character), much like the good guy PIs of TV like *Mannix* or *Barnaby Jones*.

The Scarlet King by Evan Hunter,

illo: "GH" (3500 words) ★★★

Our narrator has a problem with his temper. Whenever something irritates him, he thinks of the King of Hearts (from a deadly

Manhunt Vol. 2 No. 11 page 1 December 25, 1954. Art by Dick Sheldon.

poker game he played in the Korean War) and dispatches anyone unlucky enough to be nearby. Another minor Hunter gem with a trademark kick at the climax.

The Pickpocket by Mickey Spillane,

illo: Houlihan (1000 words) ★½

Willie's worried that his past will come back to haunt him.

Big Steal by Frank Kane,

illo: Tom O'Sullivan (8000 words) ★★

Johnny Liddell becomes involved in a stolen diamond racket when a woman asks him to hold a small package for her. When the woman ends up dead, her throat cut, and thugs rough up Johnny, Liddell enlists the aid of Inspector Herlihy to catch the "big man."

Dead Issue by Harold Q. Masur

(4000 words) ★

Scott Jordan (in his 10th

Manhunt Vol. 2 No. 11 December 25, 1954

Manhunt appearance), the lawyer who thinks he's a PI, investigates the murder of a nice old woman. The case involves the upcoming reading of a multi-million dollar will, a will that has mysteriously disappeared. A judge, admonish-ing Jordan in our opener, says, "The Assistant District Attorney tells me you have a tendency to take the law into your own hands." Indeed.

Death Sentence by Richard Deming, illo: Tom O'Sullivan (4000 words) ★★

The 10 Best Manhunt Stories of 1954
1 "Confession" by John M. Sitan (July)
2 "The Man Who Found the Money"
   by James E. Cronin (February)
3 "And Share Alike" by Charles Williams (August)
4 "Comeback" by R. Van Taylor (February)
5 "The Beatings" by Evan Hunter (October)
6 "Hit and Run" by Richard Deming (December)
7 "Pattern for Panic" by Richard S. Prather (January)
8 "A Moment's Notice" by Jerome Weidman
   (September)
9 "The Choice" by Richard Deming (June)
10 "Tin Can" by B. Traven (September)

Isobel Banner has a strange substance she wants analyzed strictly on the QT, so she hires Manville Moon to take the "strange white powder" from her. When he arrives at the party she's invited him to, he finds her dead. What was the curious substance, and why did she feel the need to keep it a secret? Moon never likes it when a potential client ends up dead before he's paid, so he takes it upon himself to find out what the mystery is. This brings up a problem with several of these PI stories—why do so many of Moon's, Jordan's, Liddell's (etc) clients seem to end up on a slab by the third page, yet they're known throughout their respective towns as guys who get the job done. Nice twist ending though!

Precise Moment by Henry Kane, illo: Houlihan (11,000 words) ★★½
Peter Chambers becomes the target of repeated gunfire after he takes part in a midnight graveyard delivery of $750,000 in ransom money. The kidnapee, the newly wed husband of multi-millionaire Florence Fleetwood Reed, may have had something to do with his own kidnapping.

Six Fingers by Hal Ellson (2000 words) ★★
The appropriately named "Six Fingers" is a very shy boy, but his friends want him to grow up fast so they involve him with a girl named Cissie.

Peter Enfantino continues to write about various horror and war comic books on <barebonesez.blogspot.com> twice weekly, covering the Warren Publishing books (*Creepy*, *Eerie*, and *Vampirella*), Atlas /Marvel pre-code horror books (*Strange Tales*, *Stories to Hold You Spellbound*, *Suspense*, *Mystic*, *Uncanny Tales*, etc.), and DC's war comics (*G.I. Combat*, *Our Army at War*, *Our Fighting Forces*, *Star Spangled War Stories*, etc).

Zymurgy for Aliens

Science Fiction by Joe Wehrle, Jr.
Illustration by Michael Neno

"Yep. My advice, get on home, climb into bed with a cold one and pull the covers over your head. There's one bad cat out on the highway."

It was just getting dark as Foley Moore's truck roared past the hitchhiker with the small suitcase, three houses from the intersection. Foley didn't even consider slowing down, not because he was only going the three houses further, but, well . . .

See, Foley had been known to ferry total strangers miles out of his way if the mood grabbed him, but not tonight .Yeah, okay, this guy was short and doughy-looking, probably couldn't break a pretzel stick in half without tools, but still, with what had been going on lately, and practically on the doorstep . . .

He swung the rusted-out Ford pickup into the gravel parking lot in front of the Thirty-six North Beer Distributor and stopped with

a sudden crunch and a spattering of stones against the Ford's underbelly.

Foley climbed out, took his baseball cap off and wiped the sleeve of his denim shirt up across his forehead, then he re-rolled the bill of the cap into a semicircle to give it just the curve he liked, pulled it back down on his shaggy head and went into the beer distributor's.

Nick Alligretti came grinning out of the stacks with a case of Yuengling and thumped it down on the counter. "Knew it was you," he said, still grinning and resting most of his bulk on an elbow.

Foley laid his last twenty and some ones on top of the case, and Nick keyed it into the register.

"Well, its a sad state of affairs when I get that predictable, Nick. It truly is." He quirked his long face to one side.

Nick chuckled. "No, no. It's your brakes I recognize. That and the rattle of rusty tin." He let go a loud guffaw.

"Yeah, that old bucket. The world won't let me get enough ahead to ditch it. I'll be drivin' that same old thing 'til it comes apart underneath me. Then I'll probably hafta bolt the sumbitch back together and keep drivin' it."

Nick raised an eyebrow. "Times is tough, man."

"Mmmn. I just passed a hitcher. You think anybody's gonna pick him up? Tonight?"

Nick snorted humorlessly. "Not me. Not you, you got any brains."

Foley nodded and trembled his shoulders for effect. "Geez, it seems like there's another body turnin' up every day or so now."

"I know. You hear about the insurance man last night?"

"*Insurance?* No. Same deal?"

"Seems like. Stark naked, dead in a ditch. Hitcher took the car and abandoned it this side of Falls Creek."

"Whoo! Getting' closer again."

"Yep. My advice, get on home, climb into bed with a cold one and pull the covers over your head. There's one bad cat out on the highway."

Foley grunted. Cold one is right. Long time since there's been anything warm in my bed, including me. "Funny thing about this guy, though, Nick. First he was goin' away from the area, now he seems to be workin' on back. Like he's lookin' for something. I wonder what the hell his agenda is?"

"You figure that out and the state cops'll set you loose in the mint. This is killin' them."

"Well, they'll get him eventually."

"Sure they will. But the attrition's gonna be terrible 'til they do."

"Yeah." Foley pocketed his change, hoisted the beer and headed for the door. "You take care, now, Nick."

Nick flapped a meaty palm at him. "Don't worry, I'll be lockin' up right after you."

Foley shoved the beer case onto the rusty bed of the pickup, took three bottles out and cradled them in his left elbow, then he fastened the tailgate up and got in behind the wheel. He pushed the bottles right under the edge of the front seat, started up, and went spinning and roaring out of the lot.

The portly hitch-hiker was nowhere in evidence, but down the road a little way a young girl stood leaning against the telephone pole, suitcase at her feet. She was wearing a flannel shirt and tight jeans.

Foley slammed the heel of his

hand against the dash. Dark as hell out, some nut killer loose in the county, and this little thing, what is she, sixteen, seventeen? just standin' there like a chicken waitin' patiently for the axe man. And all I need in *my* life is to have some state cop stop me with her inside here, try to explain that I just picked her up to save her from her own stupidity.

But he was already braking and backing up while he was thinking these things. No fool like an old . . . still, you know *somebody*'s gonna pick her up, and I pretty much know what I will or won't do, but I don't know where the next guy's head is gonna be.

The girl waited, unmoving, backbone still resting against the pole while he reached over and shoved the door open. It was too dark to see the expression on her face, but her wide eyes reflected the glow of the pickup's headlights.

"Hey, young thing. Where you headed?" As he heard himself speak, it occurred to Foley that his harsh voice and rawboned appearance might alarm her. Well, maybe a kid like her *needed* to be alarmed.

She paused, then pointed back the way he'd come.

"That way? Well, why the hell weren't you over on the other side? How far you goin'?"

"Faah?"

"Yeah. How far? You goin' far?"

She shook her head.

Foley scratched his three days beard. "Well . . . I was headed this way. But if you're really not goin' too far."

She just looked at him with those big eyes.

"Oh, man. Okay, get in."

He thought for a moment the girl didn't understand him, then she picked up her case and slowly moved to the truck. Staring at him, she climbed up into the seat and slammed the door shut. Foley gunned the old Ford into a wide U and sped off in the wrong direction for him.

As he drove, Foley reached down and pulled a bottle out from under the seat, clamped it between his legs and twisted the cap off. He raised it halfway to his mouth, stopped, and gave the girl a glance. It never felt right, drinking in front of somebody without offering. "You want one of these? Well, I know you're too young, but I don't necessarily hold to the strict letter of the law."

He held the bottle out to her, and just as he was ready to withdraw it, the girl took it. She stared at the label a long time, then she tipped it up and had a healthy swallow. She looked quizzical and examined the bottle again.

"Just don't tell anybody I gave you beer," Foley said as he opened one for himself. "Nobody's likely to stop us, anyway, out here in the sticks." The girl just gave him that wide-eyed look and took another drink.

They were several more miles along when Foley's passenger gave out an abrupt cry.

"Huh? What's wrong?"

She gesticulated wildly, indicating the side road that was coming up fast.

"Right turn? We almost there?"

"Rytrn. Rrry trn!"

Foley cut it sharp without slowing down and headed up the rise. The trees grew thicker here and the road seemed untraveled without being impassible. Foley concentrated on the unfamiliar turns until he heard the telltale sound of a bottlecap popping.

"What? You swiped another beer? You better take it easy on that stuff, kid."

The girl just looked at him and tipped the bottle up to her mouth. Foley shook his head.

After about another half mile he stopped the truck, turned on the interior light, and gave the girl his frankest attention. "You know what? I don't think we're goin' *anyplace*. Nobody's been on this road for a long time. Leastwise, not on wheels. Hikers, maybe. Now, can you understand me? Just where is it you're tryin' to go?"

She narrowed her eyes and started to say something that came out like a hiss, then she hiccuped loudly and drew back as if alarmed at her body's response to twenty-four ounces of beer.

Foley laughed, and he thought he was going to get a laugh out of her, too, the way her mouth was twitching at the corners. Then one side gaped and slanted impossibly, making the hairs on the back of his neck rise.

The girl seemed to know from his expression what had happened, but when she tried to rectify that side of her face, the other side gently melted into the features of the short dumpy-looking salesman type, last seen trying to hitch a ride down the road (Insurance salesman? *Last night's* insurance salesman, found this morning in a ditch?).

Shut up in the cab of a truck with this thing, Foley screamed, even though he'd never actually screamed before in his life. "What are you? Goddammit, don't do that to your . . . What the hell *are* you?"

Whatever she/he/it had been planning for Foley, the alcoholic disorientation had totally aborted it. Mismatched eyes gaped wide, disproportionate fingers scrabbled furiously at the door handles. It grabbed the wrong one and started winding the window up.

"Ahg ohs! Ahg ohs!" It shrieked, features momentarily wavering into those of the young gas jockey whose picture had been in the paper after his body turned up at the abandoned packing house. "Ahg ohs!"

"I'll *uggosit* for you, kid!" Foley shouted, kicking the latch with his foot. When he heard it release, he pulled back his leg for a harder thrust. "*The-door-is-uggos!*" he yelled, shoving his foot against the creature with every ounce of strength he possessed. It went toppling backward out of the truck into the weeds at the edge of the road, arms and legs flailing. Cool, fresh night air rushed into the cab.

Foley pulled the door shut, put the Ford in reverse and swung its back end into the bushes, catching his former rider in the beam of the headlights. It was struggling up awkwardly against the trunk of a large oak, body covered with twigs and dry leaf fragments. The face was now anybody's. Or nobody's. It seemed practically devoid of personality traits, except for the deepening scowl it had fixed on him. Foley turned off his interiors so it couldn't see him any more. As he jerked the transmission into drive, he wondered if zhe beer would be disruptive enough to shut the creature's systems down completely and kill it, or if it might eventually throw the toxins off and survive.

If it did . . . if it did, the repertoire of faces it had trotted out might just represent the first wave of a new peril for the world. The thing could appear as any one of a number of innocent and helpless-looking individuals, unlikely suspects. It might even change its M.O., and engage in something other than hitchhiking to accomplish whatever it was trying to accomplish, if hitching got to be too dangerous. It didn't seem to know a lot, but it was smart enough to learn.

Foley watched it a second longer as it clung dizzily to the tree trunk, then he slammed his foot down hard on the accelerator. The pickup leapt from the bushes, streaked across the dirt road and smashed the thing hard against the tree.

He pulled back a few feet and cut his motor as the broken radiator began sending pungent clouds of steam swirling up around the truck. He left the headlights burning as he got out to take a look.

The alien thing lay at the base of the tree, looking something like a squash looks a few days after you've thrown it out in the yard and it gets all pulpy and discolored and caved-in. There was a musty smell in the air. Except for the fact that the bulk of the mess was still inside the worn jeans and flannel shirt, there was little evidence that it had ever been humanoid, or could masquerade as such.

Foley watched it until he was certain it was truly dead, and wouldn't puddle up like an amoeba or reach a pseudopod or something out to snare his ankle. But no worries, the thing was done for. If they analyzed the mess, and somebody surely would, they'd likely be able to determine the nature of the thing and how much damage the beer did to it.

He went back to the truck and held the door open while he took a look at the small case, laid so carefully on the floor. It appeared very conventional at first glance, but there was no latch. Foley tried prying it open, then, more or less by accident, he applied pressure on both sides, and the two halves sprang apart.

It had more space on the inside than the outside suggested it could contain, however *that* was possible. And it was full of the clothes of all the recent murder victims. A framework of glowing blue rods in either side seemed to be what transcended conventional space and allow all the stuff to fit. It was sort of a walk-in closet in miniature.

Foley closed it up and set it on the mossy ground, wondering what the scientists would make of it. It was interesting, but there were a hell of a lot of things he needed worse than a magic suitcase.

He realized he was feeling a little shaky, so he walked back and got another beer from the beer case. Suitcase. You *could* carry a lot of beer in the magic suitcase. Yeah, but how much would it weigh, would you be carrying it all yourself, or would half the weight hang in some other dimension? Forget it. He grabbed the small sack of groceries he had in the back and tucked it in the crook of his arm so animals wouldn't get into it.

There was a flashlight up front, and a .38 in the glove compartment. He stuck the gun in the waistband of his jeans, clicked the truck lights off and the flashlight on, and headed up the road on foot. It would make for a longer hike back, but dang it, what was that thing lookin' for on such a godforsaken road? Somehow Foley just had to know.

The snap of twigs and the rattling of small stones underfoot made him nervous. What manner of ears might be listening?

The road gave out at the edge of a clearing where a trailer once stood. There was nothing of interest or value. Some discarded boards, four cement blocks, a dirty, ragged towel. But the flashlight picked out a metallic reflection through the evergreens on the slope above.

The squat, silvery vessel was settled in among the white pines. It had to have come straight down from above, otherwise it would have sheared the trees off or been damaged by them.

Foley just stood and looked at it for the longest time, moving the flashlight beam back and forth to get the whole picture cemented in his mind. Then he walked up to the rectangular seam in the metal and examined it. There was nothing to indicate it could be opened from the outside, so there had to be a trick to it. He only knew one alien word, so he said that one, but he said it in kind of a whisper, because it was embarrassing to be speaking nonsense words out loud even if there was nobody else around. "Uggos. Ug-gos."

The entire rectangle sank in six inches, then it quickly slid up inside the hull.

Oh, man. Good thing she didn't say somethin' nasty. I hope. He waited hesitantly, but nothing else happened.

Foley stepped inside a narrow, lighted passage, expecting to hear the clank of metal at his feet, but the ship's interior seemed to be coated with a neutral-colored substance which cushioned sound. As he stood there, the hatch slid shut behind him and another opened up at the end of the chamber.

Foley laid his flashlight and grocery bag down on the floor so that his right hand was free to grip the .38, while his left continued to hold the beer bottle. He crept into a large pentagonal room full of screens and unfamiliar structures that didn't quite look like either plumbing or electronics.

Beyond this confusing place he found an alcove equipped with comfortable-looking bunks and flat table-like surfaces which jutted from the wall. There didn't appear to be any sort of personal effects in sight. Foley was certain the closet-like recess beside the bunks had to be a bathroom facility, but he didn't have a clue about using the thing.

A narrow ramp led him down to a place where tables flanked a figured wall panel, and squares bearing complicated hieroglyphics glowed from a sloping board to one side. Kitchen? There was a recess in the wall panel, and Foley wondered if some utensil fitted into it, or if it might be some sort of disposal. After a moment he poured a small amount of beer into a tray in the receptacle, and was surprised when the entire frame containing the recess disappeared into the wall. One of the symbols glowed more brightly and Foley touched it to see what would happen. A minute later the section slid back out, and a chamber beside it opened, revealing a peculiar-looking mug full of pale fluid. Foley took a long, slow breath, reached for it, smelled the stuff, and after an even longer hesitation, tasted it. It was, unquestionably, chilled beer. His brand. Foley held the odd thing up to the light while he considered this phenomenon. *I think I may have something here.*

The glowing symbol paled again, but not before Foley had a chance to copy it onto the back of a tattered old card from his wallet. Then he touched the square again, just as a test. The mechanism promptly delivered another glass of excellent beer. Foley thought about his small bag of rice and cheese, black-eyed peas and salsa. Give those a spin in the old Victrola. Later.

He took both mugs and went back into what he supposed was the bridge of the ship. If only for curiosity purposes, it seemed like a good idea to find out as much as he could about the aliens. If the government got its hands on the thing, there would be precious little information forthcoming to the public.

Foley hit another glowing symbol beneath the screens, and they immediately began running concurrent information. One showed external views of an unfamiliar planet, while a second displayed what looked like three-dimensional views of (probably) its inhabitants, as seen through a break in some peculiar-looking foliage. A square on his left came glowing to life, but when Foley did nothing its light faded. He hit the screen stud again, and got a different planetary view, and different aliens. Something about these ones made him very uncomfortable, so he hit the button again. And again. And following every overview, the lighted square appeared.

He began to see a pattern. All the scenes of alien life looked like they had been captured without the subjects' knowledge, as if someone had recorded the images from a hidden vantage point. Had things like the one he killed visited all these worlds? What was their mission? Whatever it was, they didn't seem to mind wasting the locals, even for a trivial reason like obtaining convenient transportation. *Had any of their*

victims learned that you might discover or kill one with a simple brew?

Sifting through the masses of recordings, Foley eventually came across a civilization of creatures that looked a lot like Homo Sapiens, except that their ears didn't seem quite right, and their posture suggested a differently-formed pelvis. Still, they looked like nice people to Foley. He liked them at first glance. But they looked so open and vulnerable, he felt scared for them. He wondered how often and how badly they'd been preyed upon by his hitch-hiker's relatives, and he felt the heat of rage. Did they even know what they were up against? It would be good to sit down with these folks and clue them in on reality. Some people are just too damn nice for their own good.

The left-hand light came on again, and it suddenly dawned on him that its function must be to initiate course-settings for the planets onscreen. There was no other reasonable explanation. He eased his bony frame back into the recliner, let the automatic restraints close snugly around him, and reached a free finger out to depress the glowing square before the light could go off again. Foley held both beer mugs firmly against the armrests as a rising surge of clicks and hums denoted automatic inauguration of takeoff procedures. He sensed artificial gravity at his feet, and the ship begin to lift. He was still calmly watching the beer rise in the mugs when the ship cut into hyperspace.

Follow cartoonist and illustrator **Michael Neno** at <nenoworld.com>.

Beyond Understanding

Article by Vince Nowell, Sr.

"Only one issue of this magazine appeared in 1967, and it passed by all but unnoticed."

–*Science Fiction, Fantasy, and Weird Fiction Magazines* by Marshall B. Tymn and Mike Ashley Greenwood Press, 1985

Starting up a new publication is fraught with issues (no pun intended) *that endanger success—in other words it can be a "turkey shoot" proposition. Those that survive the birthing process and live to maturity do so because they are uniquely well endowed. For the rest, the handicap of inexperience and lack of quality shows up early, making one wonder, "Why did they bother in the first place?"*

Editor Horace L. Gold wrote a pep-rally treatise for the back cover of the first several issues of *Galaxy Science Fiction* magazine and *Galaxy Science Fiction Novels* entitled "You'll Never See It In Galaxy." It started out with: "Jets blasting, Bat Durston came screeching down through the atmosphere of Bbllzzaj, a tiny planet seven billion light years from Sol . . . [and so on]" The scenario was then repeated except that Bat Durston now was riding a horse on the open plains.

Gold asked his audience if they could see that that type of science fiction was merely the same as a western story, adding that *Galaxy* was many cuts above that sort of stuff because it was written for science fiction readers by authors who truly loved science fiction.

H. L. Gold's targets, as he kicked off his magazines for the Italian publishing company World Editions in 1950, were the venerable science fiction pulps, including such magazines as *Startling Stories* and *Planet Stories*. These periodicals were judged by some critics as purveyors of "space opera" and outlandish adventure stories with no real substance or well-structured plots.

In 1967, Editor Doug (Douglas) Stapleton (no biographical dates found) wrote a similar treatise

entitled "382 Words From the Editor" to kick off *Beyond Infinity* magazine. Stapleton stated, "If you're looking for bug-eyed monsters carting off well-constructed females, *Beyond Infinity* is not your meat. If you want wild, Bondian [*sic*] adventure on the outer rim of the universe, in the Black Nebula, then you'll have to look for it elsewhere." Stapleton claimed that *Beyond Infinity* was a new kind of SF publication. His publication, he said, would reach beyond to ". . . a force, a vitality, an aware aliveness [*sic*] over there in another dimen-

Douglas Stapleton, from the inside front cover of *Beyond Infinity* No. 1 Nov-Dec 1967

sion . . ." Indeed, the magazine's name carried the subtitle "Strange Tales from Other Dimensions."

As it turns out, those 382 words comprised one of the better entries in the contents for the one and only issue of this alleged bimonthly fifty-cent digest. While the goals proclaimed by Stapleton were noble, the level of the contents that followed his editorial proclamation fell sorrowfully below his objectives. Overall, the rationale for creating *Beyond Infinity*—in terms of that 382-word editorial—was *beyond understanding*.

The magazine consisted of 160 pages. The inside front cover and inside back cover were taken up by full-page b&w photo portraits of editor Stapleton, a nice looking chap, white-haired, perhaps 55–65 years old, and distinguished in appearance. There was

no caption nor any explanation for the photos. I've included a copy of the front photo here.

There was an ad for a baldness cure on page 115, one on page 137 for purchasing new cars at prices "below wholesale," and one on the back cover for an "amazing new patented invention," a spark plug that will do wonders for your car (boost gas mileage, allow quicker starts in cold or wet weather, etc.). Yet there was a quantity of blank space on some pages at the ends of stories.

But amazingly—for a new publication—there were no ads pushing subscriptions. For that matter, the contents page indicia made no mention of subscriptions, only instructions for submitting manuscripts. There was nothing about any forthcoming issues, stories or authors. Typically such information appears in a first issue to help attract readers (buyers) and get them to search for the next issue.

All illustrations were done by Lynn Goller, whose name is listed on the contents page. Many of these were printed in two colors (black plus a second). The style was sketchbook, with the art sometimes simply tossed around on the page. And then appears—on page 71—a full-page b&w sketched portrait of Abraham Lincoln printed with a red background. No caption, no reason. Nice, but irrelevant!

The contents page—reproduced here—displays another anomaly. The story contents are not listed in page order, nor in title/author alphabetical order, nor in logical groupings such as novelettes versus short stories. They're simply listed—and order be damned!

Yet another oddity: at the title

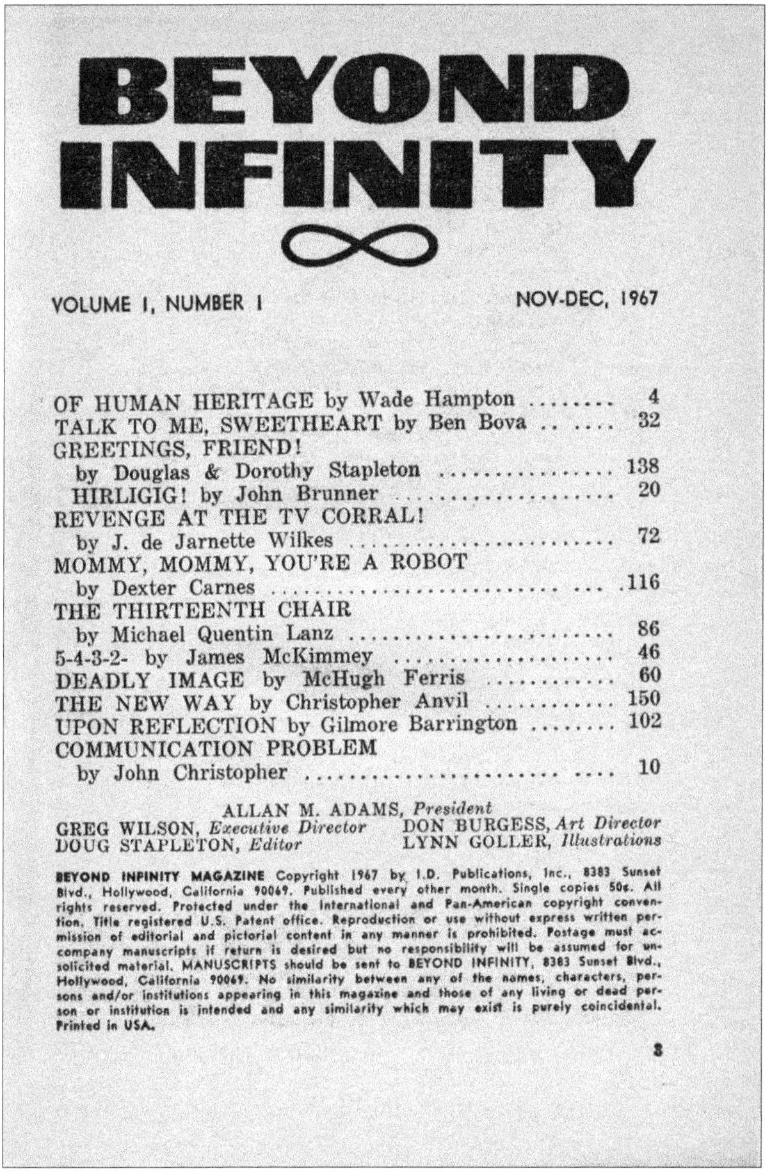

BEYOND INFINITY

∞

VOLUME 1, NUMBER 1 **NOV-DEC, 1967**

ALLAN M. ADAMS, *President*
GREG WILSON, *Executive Director*   DON BURGESS, *Art Director*
DOUG STAPLETON, *Editor*   LYNN GOLLER, *Illustrations*

BEYOND INFINITY MAGAZINE Copyright 1967 by I.D. Publications, Inc., 8383 Sunset Blvd., Hollywood, California 90069. Published every other month. Single copies 50¢. All rights reserved. Protected under the International and Pan-American copyright convention. Title registered U.S. Patent office. Reproduction or use without express written permission of editorial and pictorial content in any manner is prohibited. Postage must accompany manuscripts if return is desired but no responsibility will be assumed for unsolicited material. MANUSCRIPTS should be sent to BEYOND INFINITY, 8383 Sunset Blvd., Hollywood, California 90069. No similarity between any of the names, characters, persons and/or institutions appearing in this magazine and those of any living or dead person or institution is intended and any similarity which may exist is purely coincidental. Printed in USA.

3

page beginning of each new story *there are no author(s) named.* One has to refer back to the contents page to see who wrote the story. At the end of every story appears a circular symbol with the word "End" upside down. It's all *beyond rational explanation.*

The publisher is identified as I.D. Publications, Inc., with a corporate president, an executive director, and so on. Of the five managerial personages listed on the contents page, I could only find data on the editor and the art personnel, and damned little of that. Art Director Don Bur-

gess may be the same Don Burgess who specializes in sports pictures, especially of hockey players. There is a California illustrator named Lynn Goller who gets cover-artist credit in the ISFDB (International Speculative Fiction Database), but I could not discover any details about her.

Editor Doug (as Douglas) Stapleton is credited with two published short stories under his name alone in the 1942 pulp magazine issues of *Jungle Stories* and *Thrilling Wonder Stories*. Then, co-authoring with his (assumed) wife Dorothy, there was another short story in a 1954 *Thrilling Wonder Stories*, a December 1959 short story in *Future Science Fiction* (No. 46), and the novelette, in this issue of *Beyond Infinity* in 1967.

Stapleton also edited another one-shot magazine for I.D. Publications entitled *Whodunit?* which made its solo appearance in October 1967. I do not have a copy and decided not to spend $10 to acquire a used issue after I had read *Beyond Infinity*.

There also is an interesting footnote about I.D. Publications' office location at the end of this article, but first let's take a look at the authors and story contents of *Beyond Infinity*. Of the 12 stories' authors' names, there are no data on these six: Wade Hampton, J. de Jarnette Wilkes, Dexter Carnes, Michael Quentin Lanz, McHugh Ferris, and Gilmore Harrington. Editor Stapleton's novelette (with co-author Dorothy Stapleton), "Greetings, Friend!" is probably the best fiction out of the dozen total in the issue.

Doug Stapleton alone is also the author of a mass-market paperback book, *Debbie Preston, Teenage Reporter, in The Case of the Superstar Mystery Cruise* published by New American Library in 1973. (See cover illustration showing a young Donnie Osmond on the right in the cover photo.) Copies are available from Amazon for $120! But why? It's *beyond belief*.

A "Doug Stapleton" is also credited by Amazon as a co-author of a catalog for an exhibition at the Ukrainian Institute of Modern Art held in Chicago in 2014. The catalog title is *Morris Barazani: Shoots Straight, 1948–2014*, published by Corbett vs. Dempsey [*sic*] in 2014. The date and Stapleton's likely age in 1967 make this credit dubious. But back to *Beyond Infinity*.

There is a C+-grade short story entitled "5-4-3-2-" by James Mc Kimmey (1923–2011). He is the author of a number of mystery books plus a story in *IF Worlds of Science Fiction* (November 1953).

"Talk to Me, Sweetheart," the Ben Bova (b. 1932) story by the former editor of *Analog Science Fact/Fiction* is disappointing. This well-known, award-winning author usually does much higher quality work than in this piece. This one may have been salvaged from a much earlier slush pile.

Superstar Mystery Cruise 1973

Whodunit? No. 1 October 1967

John Brunner (1934–1995), a well-known, award-winning British SF writer of novels and short stories, was the author of an awkward story about jazz (I think) in a story titled "Whirligig!" That's the spelling used on the story's title page. In the Table of Contents, the "W" is missing. [Like the comedian wrote, "They shoulda hired me as poofreader!" {*sic*}]

Brunner, incidentally, is credited with inventing the space/time universe term "worm" (as applied to spatial wormholes), and further predicted the emergence of computer viruses in his 1975 novel, *The Shockwave Rider*.

Christopher Anvil (1925–2009) is a pseudonym for the American author Harry Christopher Crosby. His SF career began, under his own name, with the story "Cinderella, Inc." in the December 1952 issue of William Hamling's *Imagination* magazine (started by Raymond A.

Palmer in 1950). By 1956 he was appearing in the revered *Astounding Science Fiction* under his adopted pen name. He appeared in *Beyond Infinity* with the story "The New Way," a stretched-out tale about corporal punishment in the future.

John Christopher's catchy "Communication Problem" is the second piece of fiction in *Beyond Infinity* but appears last on the contents page. Christopher (Sam Youd, 1922–2012) was a familiar British name in SF circles. His novel *The Death of Grass*, also published as *No Blade of Grass* (1956), was made as a film starring Nigel Davenport and produced by Cornel Wilde. [Are any of you readers old enough to quickly recognize these names?] Christopher also published stories under a variety of pen names.

The stories by the six unknown writers make up about 40% of the issue but do not merit descriptions here. However, one of those authors—"Dexter Carnes"—is the same name used for a character in a book for young girls. Could that book be the Debbie Preston mystery novel by Doug Stapleton?

As promised, there is a footnote to this article. It concerns the address for I.D. Publications: 8383 Sunset Blvd. in Hollywood, California. That address was a long-time nightclub in the area known as the Sunset Strip, a stretch of boulevard with famous entertainment spots, such as Ciro's. Today it lies within the largely LGBTQ community of the incorporated city of West Hollywood.

The night spots along the strip were famous for brawls and fistfights that included such stars as Frank Sinatra. The first club at 8383 Sunset Blvd. opened in 1934 as Café Clement, featuring "European cuisine" (French-Italian), a cocktail lounge, and dancing. In 1936 Martha Raye, at the top of her form, appeared there, along with a variety of other acts. The club changed its name to Club Casanova during her stint. Later (1937) it transformed into "U-Gene's Bagdad," with a "Harlem in Hollywood" theme. It advertised as ". . . Harlem brought right to Hollywood's front door with an all-star colored revue . . ." [Try such promo wording today!] The cover charge was $5.00 per person.

On July 6, 1939, 8383 Sunset Blvd. made its bow as "Little Eva." It featured dinners priced at $1.50 and Suppers for 75¢. Entertainment was by the Dick Haynes Orchestra for dancing. Shortly after this, in October 1939, the address became "The Sports Circle." By May 1940 it was a real estate office, and after

1943 a failed carpet business.

In January 1949 it once again was operated as a nightclub, the "Club Casanova" (See photo.) Its claim-to-fame was the so-called "Battle of Sunset Strip" involving gangster Mickey Cohen and unknown foes, that began at Club Casanova as a fight between club manager Leo Pavich and a wealthy playboy/race-car driver/stuntman/pilot named Joel W. Thorne. The case went to court but ended in a mistrial. I mention this because Thorne was killed at age 40 in October 1955 when his airplane crashed into a North Hollywood apartment building on Magnolia Blvd. The crash killed eight people in a second-floor apartment where a family was celebrating the baptism of a baby.

On that autumn night I ran outside our North Hollywood home two miles north of Magnolia Blvd. when I heard a plane flying very low to the ground over our house, heading south. When I went to school the next morning (I was a senior), I discovered that the plane I'd heard had crashed across the street from North Hollywood High School. There was speculation at that time that pilot Thorne was drunk and suicidal.

So 18 years after Club Casanova opened, the address of 8383 Sunset Blvd. was the short-lived home of I.D. Publications, Inc. Viewed from today's perspective, the physical location—along with the two titles produced there—*Beyond Infinity* and *Whodunit?*—all seem *beyond believability*.

"It's okay. The streetlights are LED. It'll take a while for them to brighten up."

Paperback Parade No. 104
Review by Richard Krauss

"This issue I am proud to present a look at the American paperbacks of Carter Brown, and the cover art on those books by Robert McGinnis, Baryé Phillips and others."

Gary Lovisi, *Paperback Parade* No. 104 August 2019

Paperback Talk

Gary Lovisi shares the latest from indie publishers like Stark House, Wildside, Justin Marriott, Dan Zimmer, Audrey Parente, and many others; along with comments on Tom Lesser's annual Paperback Show in Glendale. Greg Ketter sent cover images from five different novels published about 1945 that use the same cover artwork. Ernest Spainhower contributes a few more "mean dog" covers including one by Raymond Chandler: *Killer in the Rain* from Ballantine. Lovisi's "Paperback Talk" is always a fun read.

Carter Brown: The Writer & the Stories

Art Scott's bio piece on Alan G. Yates, who went on to write over 300 novels as bestselling author Carter Brown (CB). Scott includes highlights of Yates' career from his autobiography, *Ready When You Are, CB!*

CB: The Books & the Covers

Art Scott turns his attention to Brown's cover artists in the next feature; first to Baryé Phillips, and then Robert McGinnis. Both artists are well represented with over a dozen cover repros each, before trends shifted and Signet replaced art with photography.

CB: The Signet List

Gary Lovisi and Art Scott teamed up to compile a list of the American Signet editions of Carter Brown's paperbacks, noting which character stars in each one: Larry Baker, Rick Holman, Al Wheeler, Danny Boyd, Mavis Seidlitz, Randy Roberts, Paul Donovan, Andy Kane, or Mike Farrel; and its cover artist. With still more full-color covers sprinkled throughout the list, Gary and Art have created an essential resource for collectors.

CB: Belmont-Tower

Wrapping up this special Carter Brown section of *Paperback Parade*, Art Scott provides the backstory—and a checklist—of the Belmont-Tower library; twelve editions, published in 1979–1981. Thankfully, only four are shown with their repetitive bulls-eye target motif.

Fearn's Jinxed Novels

Philip Harbottle solves a 30-year-old mystery as he uncovers the truth behind Gannet Press'

Son of Dick Turpin and *Turpin's Son Rides Again*, complete with printing antics uncannily akin to those described by Steve Carper in "A Classic Error" on page 124. Harbottle's piece is illustrated by a very nice collection of UK covers.

Matchless Paperbacks: *Straw Boss*

Richard Greene never ceases to amaze me with his feature on promotional matchbooks for paperbacks—although in this issue he's put out a request to readers for pulps and PBs that include matchbooks on their covers, so perhaps he'll explore a new angle on this soon. But this time, he shines the spotlight on *Straw Boss* by Stephen Longstreet with a rare matchbox depicting its cover.

Mighty Midgets

Even a lifelong collector and bookseller like Gary Lovisi can manage to run across a series he's never seen before. In this case, Mighty Midgets, a series of 60 small British pre-vintage era paperbacks. Illustrating his article are well over a dozen covers and a complete checklist.

Early Penguin Science Fiction

"Penguin revolutionized publishing in the 1930s through its inexpensive paperbacks, sold through Woolworths and other stores for pennies—bringing high-quality paperback fiction and non-fiction to the mass market." Jon D. Swartz highlights the company's many science fiction titles and authors in this informative article.

Bill Crider

A brief, heart-felt tribute to the Alvin, Texas author of several

series, and dozens of stories spanning every genre. Jon D. Swartz includes a great photo of Bill, seated at his computer, doing what he loved best: writing stories.

Summary

This issue provides another fascinating foray into the world of collectible paperback books. The emphasis is on Carter Brown and his American paperbacks, but there's enough ink on other series to delight nearly any collector.

Paperback Parade No. 104 Aug. 2019
Editor: Gary Lovisi
Designer: Richard Greene
~5.5" x 8.5" 100 pages, full color throughout
$15 + postage for a single issue
$40 for three-issue subscription
<gryphonbooks.com>

Paul D. Marks

From the author's <SleuthSayers.org> introduction

I'm old enough to have grown up in Los Angeles when both Raymond Chandler's L.A. and Chandler himself were still around. When I was a kid L.A. still resembled the city of Chandler's "mean streets," Ross MacDonald's Lew Archer and Cain's *Double Indemnity*. In fact, I grew up in a Spanish-style house very much like the one that Barbara Stanwyck lives in in the movie version of *Double Indemnity*.

L.A. was a film noir town for a film noir kid. And that certainly had an influence on me and my writing. And a lot of my writing involves L.A., not just as a location but almost as a character in its own right. Of course, we're all influenced by our childhoods, where we grew up and the people we knew. And those things, whether

conscious or unconscious, tend to bubble to the surface in our writing like the black pitch bubbling up from the La Brea tar pits.

Two things that Los Angeles means to me are movies and noir, oh, and palm trees, of course. Movie studios and backlots were everywhere in this city. You couldn't help but see the studios, feel their presence and be influenced by "the movies" one way or another. Many of the studios and backlots are gone now, but almost everywhere you go in this city is a movie memory and often a noir memory. L.A. is Hollywood's backlot and many films, including many noirs, were filmed throughout the city.

As a kid, a teenager and even a young adult, I experienced many of the places I read about in books and saw in the movies, once the movies got out of the backlot and onto those mean L.A. streets. Not as a tourist, but as part of my "backyard."

So Los Angeles has insinuated itself into my writing. Here's some examples of how it might have gotten there and how it reflects my view of the ironically named City of Angels.

Angels Flight is a funicular railway in downtown Los Angeles. Star of many films and many noirs, including *Kiss Me, Deadly, Criss Cross* and others. Chandler visits it in *The High Window* and *The King in Yellow*. As a young boy, my dad took me to the original Angels Flight (now moved down the road and since closed). And though I may not have known about noir films and hardboiled novels then, it was an experience I've always remembered. Such a cool little pair of trains going up and down that hill, the tracks splitting in the

Angels Flight Timeless Skies Publishing, 2015

middle just as each car approaches the other and you think they're going to smash into each other head on. Angels Flight slams back to me in memory every now and then and makes its way into my writing, most notably in the eponymous story *Angels Flight*, which I must say came out before Michael Connelly's novel of the same name.

That story, about a cop whose time has come and gone, is still pretty relevant today. The world is changing and he's having one hell of a time catching up, if he even wants to. He's a dinosaur. And he knows that Angels Flight is an anachronism, just like he is. He says to the other main character:

Will Angels Flight bring back the glamour of the old days? Hollywood's lost its tinsel. Venice's lost its pier. And there are no angels in the City

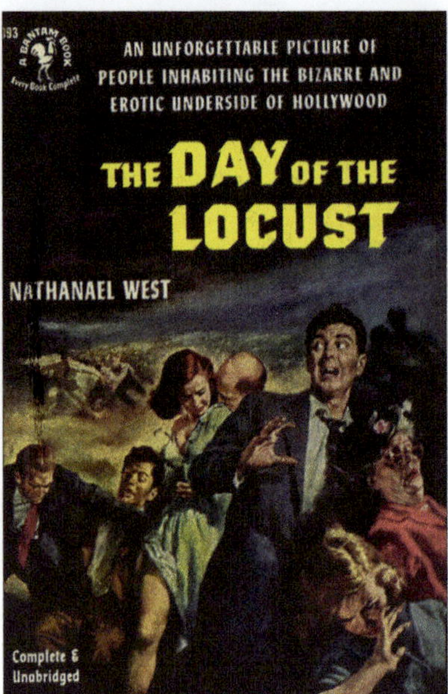

The Day of the Locust by Nathanael West
Bantam Books No. 1093, 1953

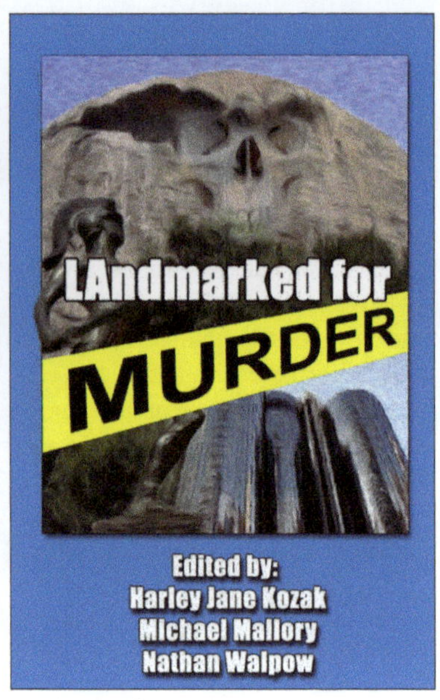

LAndmarked for Murder
with Marks'"Sleepy Lagoon Nocturne"
Top Publications, 2009

of Angels. What can Angels Flight do to bring that back?"

"Sometimes you need something for the soul," the other person says.

I think that sums up a lot of my attitude not only toward Angels Flight but to the City of Angels as well.

In Nathanael West's *Day of the Locust*, Tod Hackett comes to L.A. thinking he's an artist. And like so many others he gets trampled by that dream. Not much has changed all these decades later in my story "Endless Vacation," when a young woman comes to Hollywood with big dreams and a bigger heroin habit. The narrator tries to help but he also knows:

Who the hell am I to talk? I came to L.A. looking for a Hollywood that died before I was born. A glamorous town of mov-ie stars and studios and backlots. A studio system that nurtured talent, whatever you say about how it also might have stifled it with the other hand. A town that made movies in black and white but whose streets were, indeed, paved with gold. Yeah, I bought it—hook, line and clapboard.

Luis Valdez examines the Zoot Suit Riots that took place in L.A. during World War II in his play *Zoot Suit*. I remember my grandfather, who lived through that time, talking about "pachucos" when I was a kid. In my story "Sleepy Lagoon Nocturne," set during the war, I take a stab at dealing with the racial tension of that era.

Hot jazz—swing music— boogied, bopped and jived. And Bobby Saxon was one of those who made it happen. Bobby banged the eighty-eights with the Booker "Boom-Boom" Taylor Orchestra in the Club Alabam down on Central Avenue. It was the heppest place for whites to come slumming and mix with the coloreds. That's just the way it was in those days, Los Angeles in the 1940s during the war.

Venice Beach and boardwalk is the number one tourist destination in Los Angeles. People think it's cool and flock to see the "freaks," and maybe the nearby Venice Canals. Developer Abbott Kinney wanted to recreate Italy's Venice in L.A., and he did, to some extent. But it didn't quite work out. Many of the canals were drained and filled in, though some remain. They can be seen in several movies, too numerous to name. And, because they were another place I'd *done time* at, they pop up in my short story "Santa Claus Blues," which opens with a bunch of kids playing along the canals and coming across a dead Santa floating in one of them.

Staring at the canal, Bobby thought about Abbott Kinney's dream for a high culture theme park, with concerts, theatre and lectures on various subjects. Kinney even imported Italian gondoliers to sing to visitors as they were propelled along the canals. When no one seemed to care about the highbrow culture he offered he switched gears and turned Venice into a popular amusement area. And finally the people came.

My grandparents always referred to MacArthur Park, on Wilshire Boulevard on the way to downtown, as Westlake Park, its original name. It was renamed for General Douglas MacArthur after World

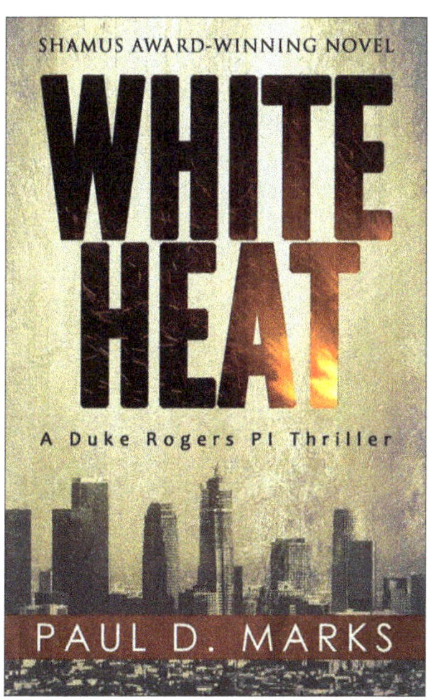

White Heat Down & Out Books, 2018

War II. But for my grandparents it was always Westlake. When I was a kid it was the place they took me to have a picnic and rent a boat and paddle around the lake. A nice outing. In the movies it's the scene of a murder in one of my favorite obscure noirs, *Too Late for Tears.* By the time of my novel *White Heat*, set during the 1992 "Rodney King" riots, the *nature* of the park had changed from when I was a kid:

MacArthur Park is midway between Hancock Park, not a park, but an upper class neighborhood, and downtown L.A., a neighborhood in search of an identity. When I was a boy, my grandparents used to take me to the park. We'd rent rowboats and paddle through the lake, tossing bread crumbs to the birds. The park is a different place today. You can still rent

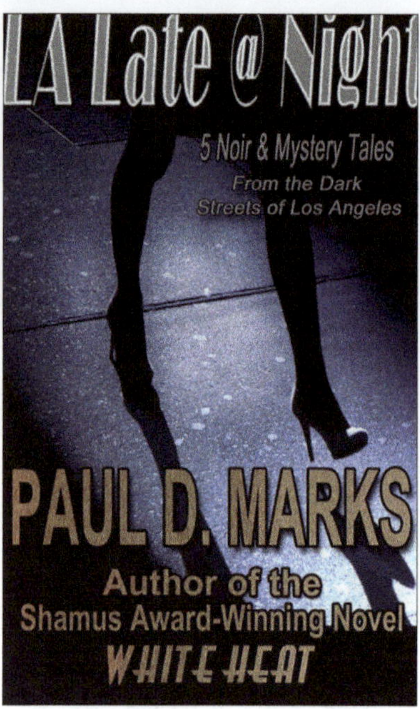

LA Late @ Night Timeless Skies Publishing 2014

paddle boats—if you want to paddle across the lake while talking to your dealer. Sometimes on Saturdays or Sundays immigrant families still try to use it as a park. Most of the time, it's a haven for pushers, crack addicts, hookers and worse. Even the police don't like treading there. If they were scared, who was I to play Rambo?

Even if someone's never been to Los Angeles, most people know Sunset Boulevard and the Sunset Strip. Sunset begins or ends, depending on how you look at it, at Pacific Coast Highway on the west and continues to Union Station in downtown L.A., though recently the last part of the jog has been renamed. It goes from wealthy homes in Santa Monica and the West Side, into Beverly Hills, through the Strip in West Hollywood, where hippies back in the day and hipsters today hang out. Into Hollywood and on to downtown. It's a microcosm of Los Angeles. Of course, both Union Station and Sunset have made multiple appearances in movies and novels and have made several appearances in my writing. Sunset was a major artery in my life as well as in the city. One time I walked almost the entire length of Sunset on a weekend day with my dad, ending up at Union Station. Later, I hung on the Strip. I drove it to the beach. I slammed through the road's Dead Man's Curve, made famous in the Jan and Dean song. Sunset appears in my stories "Born Under a Bad Sign," "Dead Man's Curve," "L.A. Late @ Night" and more. In the latter, Sunset is as much of a character in the story as any of the human characters.

She'd only noticed the mansion. Not long after that, her parents had taken her to the beach. They had driven Sunset all the way from Chavez Ravine to the ocean. She had seen houses like the one in the movie. Houses she vowed she'd live in some day.

What she hadn't realized at the time was that there was a price to pay to be able to live in such a house. Sometimes that price was hanging from a tag that everyone can see. Sometimes it was hidden inside.

And who doesn't know the famous—or infamous—Hollywood Sign? Something I saw almost every day as a kid, and which a friend of mine and I hiked up to many, many years ago, before it was all fenced in and touristy. In "Free Fall," originally published in Gary Lovisi's *Hardboiled* magazine, a man recently separated from the service, heads west, as far west as he can go until he comes to the terminus of Route 66 in Santa Monica, near the Santa Monica Pier. This is the end of the road for him in more ways than one.

I kept looking at the Hollywood Sign, wondering about all the people down below, pretending to be in its glow. Where do they go after L.A.? There is nowhere, the land ends and they just tumble into the arroyos and ravines, never to be heard from again.

So this is a sampling of my writing and my relationship to L.A., La La Land, the City of the Angels, the Big Orange. Could I have written about these places without experiencing them? Sure. We can't experience everything we write about. But hopefully it has made my writing more authentic. Maybe there are other cities less well traveled that would be ripe for exploration in movies and books. Maybe L.A. is overworked and overdone. But Los Angeles is part of me. Part of who I am. So it's not only a recurring locale in my writing, it's a recurring theme. And I've only just touched the surface here of Los Angeles, the city, its various landmarks and neighborhoods and my relationship to it.

So that's part of what shaped me and makes me who I am. And some of my L.A. story. You can take the boy out of L.A., but you can't take L.A. out of the boy.

Paul D. Marks

Interviewed by Richard Krauss

The Digest Enthusiast: "Ghosts of Bunker Hill" opens with a murder—the murder of its narrator Kevin Birch—who tells the story from the afterlife. His old friend, PI Howard Hamm, is hired by his widow, Nicole, to find out who done it. The story received the 2016 *EQMM* Readers Award.

The first Howard Hamm story, "Ghosts of Bunker Hill," ends soundly without much hint there's more to come. When did you decide you had a series on your hands?

Paul D. Marks: Every time I write something I slam my fist down and say, "this is not going to be a series." The reason being that I worry that the characters will grow stale. How much can you do with one or two people from book to book/ story to story, especially if it goes over several books or short stories? But then I get infatuated with the characters, they intrigue me. I see facets of them I didn't realize were there before I started writing. And I want to explore those more, so I come up with another story in which to explore those aspects of the characters. With the Bunker Hill series it was just too good of an idea to let it slide in a single outing. The fact that it received the *EQMM* Readers

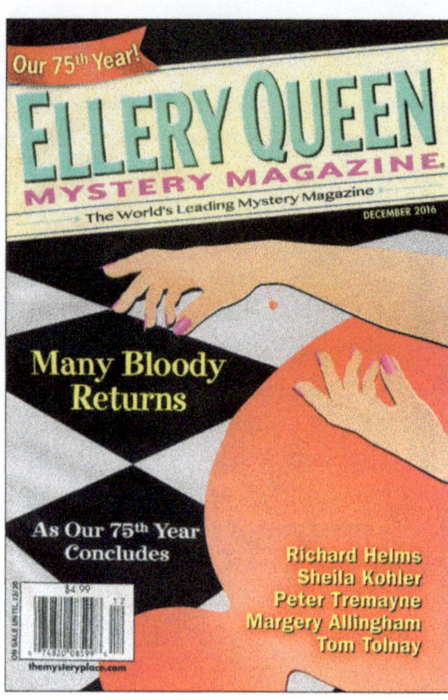

EQMM December 2016 with Marks' "Ghosts of Bunker Hill" Cover by Jill Hartley

Award (and my wife and I went to NYC to receive that and go with the Ellery Queen team to the Edgars) certainly didn't hurt in terms of wanting to continue with the series. But the same thing happened with Duke Rogers, from my novels *White Heat* and *Broken Windows*. Initially I didn't want to write a sequel to *White Heat*, but the characters intrigued me, both Duke and his very unPC partner, Jack. Those novels are different in tone (more hardboiled) from the Bunker Hill stories. They're set in the 1990s and there's a lot of events that took place then that can be a prism for viewing things happening today. In *White Heat* it's the Rodney King riots and racism, in *Broken Windows*, immigration and California's infamous anti-illegal alien Proposition 187. So there's always more to explore.

I don't always start off thinking that something will be or would make a good series. I have a novel coming out next year—*The Blues Don't Care*—that's set in Los Angeles during WWII with a very unique and interesting lead character. I was thinking that might end up becoming a series, especially since that character is in three published short stories, though they came out a long time ago. And when I wrote my short story "Windward," that won the Macavity Award and was selected for the *Best American Mysteries of 2018*, I wasn't thinking series. But now I'm thinking maybe it should go that way, so never say never.

TDE: How did your idea of a ghost and a PI "partnership" germinate?

PDM: People often ask where your ideas come from. They just sort of come out of the air. You might hear or see something on TV or in a magazine that sparks an idea and you take it from there. Or you overhear a snatch of conversation. I was in a famous L.A. bar one time—Barney's Beanery—when two guys got in a fight at a pool table. I ended up using that in something. Steve Jobs and Steve Wozniak created tech ideas out of the air and I create story ideas the same way. I couldn't do what they do and I'm not sure if they could do what I do.

I've always been fascinated by the Bunker Hill area of Los Angeles. And if you watch film noirs you've seen it plenty of times in movies like *Criss Cross*, *Kiss Me, Deadly*, *The Brasher Doubloon* and *Cry Danger*. One of my favorite L.A. writers, John Fante, lived there and wrote about it. It started out as a swanky area near downtown L.A., but got run down around World War I to the point that Raymond Chandler called it "shabby town." So I wanted to do something set there, but there is no there there anymore. The area was redeveloped to the point that it's unrecognizable today. But a lot of the Victorian mansions were moved to Carrol Avenue a few miles away. I liked that setting and the idea of the "ghosts" of Bunker Hill—ghosts in more ways than one. So now I needed a P.I. and Howard Hamm was born, along with his best friend Kevin Birch. I didn't want Howard to have the standard sidekick, not that there's anything wrong with that, and because Bunker Hill and Carroll Avenue and the like are filled with "ghosts," nostalgia and relics of the past, I thought maybe Howard's partner should be a ghost.

TDE: How would you describe the POV of "Ghosts," and what special challenges did it present?

PDM: The POV issue in the Ghosts of Bunker Hill stories, especially after the first one is a bit of a problem. The way I see it, Kevin, the ghostly narrator, is an omniscient observer of the action. But, much as he wants to help Howard out he has no way to communicate with him through the astral plane. Which is frustrating for him when he sees things that could help his friend out. It's kind of like in the movies when kids see the bad guy hiding behind the door and yell at the screen for the characters to watch out. They can yell, but the characters don't hear them and that's Kevin's frustration. As for Kevin playing less of a key part in the subsequent stories, I think that's a natural progression because he can no longer be intrinsically involved in the plots since he's in another dimension. But he does narrate all the stories and relates things about Howard that we might otherwise not know.

TDE: Why did you decide to make your PI, Howard Hamm, African American? How do keep his ethnicity authentic?

PDM: Things like this are very touchy these days. But I wanted Howard and his best friend, Kevin, to be from different backgrounds, different parts of Los Angeles, but sharing certain commonalities, while at the same time having different perspectives. And, while people do have different experiences, we are all Americans and are all steeped in American culture to one degree or another. We have more in common than whatever separates us. If I was to write only what I am or what I've experienced I couldn't write women characters or private detectives, since I've never been those things. I couldn't write stuff set in the 1940s during World War II since I wasn't there then. And other people couldn't write white males or whatever else they might not be or have experienced. I doubt George Lucas has been to outer space, so should he not write *Star Wars* because he hasn't experienced it? So again, we have to use our commonality as people, and our experiences of knowing people of different backgrounds. Plus, many of my characters are based on people I know or have known over the years. So Howard has things in common with several people that I've known. That's how I try to keep him authentic. And, writing is about imagination. About putting yourself in another person's shoes. If we can't write characters who are different than us, then we can't write.

One of my favorite movies is

EQMM Sep/Oct *2017* with Marks'"Bunker Hill Blues" Cover by Christine Marie Larson

Ghost World, with Thora Birch, Scarlett Johansson and Steve Buscemi. It's about two teenaged girls graduating high school and starting their life journeys. To paraphrase the old House on Un-American Activities question, I am not now nor have I ever been a teenaged girl. Yet I totally relate to this movie and these characters and their alienation. Why? Because what they're going through is universal. It's the same with writing a black character or anyone else. You have to try to relate to their humanity. We empathize, we put ourselves in others' shoes. And we do the best we can.

And you know what—I'm not a ghost (at least I don't think I am). Yet I write a ghost character. And no one that I know of is a ghost. I don't know anyone to even ask what a ghost's experience is like. So I have to make it up based on pure speculation and imagination.

TDE: I follow you on Sleuthsayers.org and Facebook, you're obviously a big fan of noir films and fiction, which colors your stories. How do you balance nostalgic references with narrative drive?

PDM: It's definitely a balancing act trying to keep the narrative driving forward while adding a little color to the stories. One of the things I find I miss in a lot, though not all, newer mystery/crime fiction is that feeling of atmosphere and place that Raymond Chandler did so well. And I like my stories to be set in a specific place, not some generic city that could be anywhere. So I try to add things that will give the reader a feel for that place or time, if the story's set in a different time. The best way to do that and keep the narrative drive going is to have those things tie into the story. So in "Fade-Out on Bunker Hill" (the third Bunker Hill story in the March/April 2019 issue of *EQMM*), I might talk about Sunset Boulevard (both the street and the movie) or the Whitley Heights neighborhood and give some background on them, but within the context of the story. Sometimes, I admit, I take a side trip, like a mini prose Sunday drive, to talk about a location like Angels Flight in "Ghosts of Bunker Hill." But I hope they're things that ultimately add to the story and give the readers a more immersive experience, while not taking away too much from that forward momentum.

Another thing I like to do is show how things in the past are reflections of things happening today. How the past influences the present. For example, in "Ghosts of Bunker Hill," the ghost interacts with *ghosts* of L.A.'s literary past—Phillip Marlowe and Arturo Bandini, who aren't even ghosts of real people. They're ghosts of fictional characters. But they're literary figures who have defined our image of Los Angeles. In a way they've shaped how we view L.A. today. Things change over time, but the human experience, love, hate, fear, murder and greed never change.

TDE: The second story, "Bunker Hill Blues," opens with Kevin Birch's first person narrative from the afterlife, then slides into his third person perspective and stays there. A long-ago former occupant of Kevin's old Victorian, now owned by PI Howard Hamm, stops by and asks for a nostalgic peek at the old place. Hamm obliges, they get to talking, and before long the woman wants to hire him to track down her brother, whom she hasn't seen for decades.

What inspired this particular story and how did you go about writing it?

PDM: I've often thought about going back to the house I grew up in, a sort of Spanish Revival similar to Barbara Stanwyck's house in *Double Indemnity*. I drive by it often and think, what would happen if I stopped and knocked on the door? Would they think I'm nuts? Would they invite me in? Would they shoot me? So I think that might have been the genesis for that story.

All houses have memories. Of the people who lived there before. The "ghosts"—not in the Casper or *Ghostbusters* supernatural way, but in the memories of the people who lived there. When my wife and I were looking for houses we looked at one where someone had committed suicide. We really wanted that house and, obviously, it had some history to it. Ultimately we didn't get it but not for that reason. But it did make us think twice about if we really wanted to live somewhere where something so tragic happened?

It's like the expression 'if these walls could talk'. So using that as jumping off point, I wondered what the walls, or to be more specific in the case of "Bunker Hill Blues," the floors, could talk to Howard about. He notices some initials carved in the floor and then one of the people whose initials they are shows up at his door. And from there you have the jumping off point for a story. Which, since I write mysteries and thrillers, will involve a crime that Howard will help to solve.

I'm a "pantster," which means I write by the seat of my pants. I start with an idea and then just start writing and let my characters "walk and talk". Sometimes the outcome surprises me. I don't always know exactly where the story is going until I start writing it. I hate outlining. It stifles my creativity trying to think ahead in that format. I think the more interesting aspects of the story come out when you're just letting it flow. When you have an outline I think it keeps your mind from thinking outside of the parameters of the outline. Kind of like coloring inside the lines—I like to *color* outside the lines. The closest I get to an outline is that I will sometimes write my first draft as a screenplay with very little description, just dialog and action. Then I'll flesh that out into a full blown story or novel.

And re: short story vs. novel: I think they're different, but I think they're more the same than different. Each needs a beginning, middle and end.

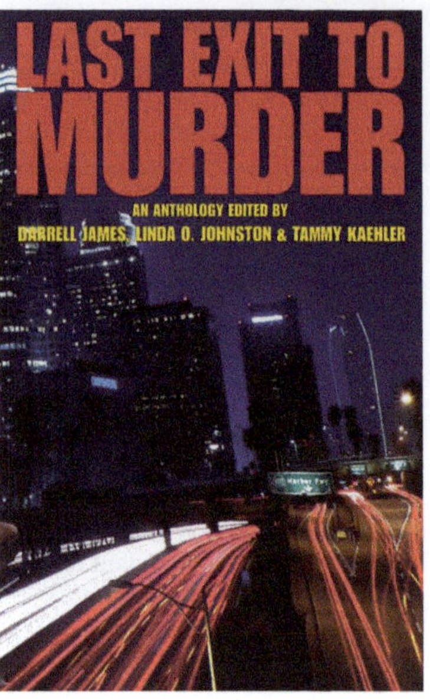

EQMM Mar/Apr *2019* with Marks'"Fade-Out on Bunker Hill." Cover by Chris Clor.

Last Exit to Murder with Marks'"Dead Man's Curve" Down & Out Books, 2013

Short stories are like single records, 45s, remember those? They're short and probably should be catchy. Have a hook. Short stories are more challenging in some ways. You have to say more in less space. In short stories, I concentrate more on the characters than the story or the who-dunit. To me, the who-dunit/how-dunit is less important than creating a compelling character that people can relate to and care about, even if they're anti-heroes and maybe not the most upstanding citizens. In my story "Dead Man's Curve," the character is a burned out musician who's duped into carrying a dead body in the trunk of a car. And, while you do find out who duped him and how, the parts of the story I like best are the parts where we learn about him and how he got to the state he's in. I was afraid the editors of the anthology (*Last Exit to Murder*) would want to cut out all that stuff, but happily they didn't. That's where we really get to know him, who he is, how he got down and out, what his dreams were and are today.

Novels are more like symphonies. You have an overture, where you introduce the main themes and then you explore those themes in more depth. And in novels you have a different problem: keeping the momentum going throughout the story. You have more space and room to explore the characters situations, and settings, but you can't let that drag the story down and keep it from unfolding and moving forward. You also have time to go off on different tangents, explore different possibilities and more characters.

But ultimately both forms come down to having interesting characters with problems that need to be overcome. Some people like a twist at the end of a short story, and that's fine if it works for the story, but to me the main element is the character and how they resolve—or don't resolve—their issues.

TDE: The third story, "Fade-Out on Bunker Hill," is about a remake of *Sunset Boulevard* in which the lead actress is murdered. What's the background on this one?

PDM: As you mention above, I love old movies and film noir in particular. I also love (well love-hate) Los Angeles, my hometown. So riffing on Billy Wilder's *Sunset Boulevard* seemed like a natural for me. The story's opening mimics the opening of *Sunset Boulevard*, but in the case of "Fade-Out on Bunker Hill," Howard finds an actress floating face down in a hot tub instead of William Holden floating face down in a swimming pool. And, while Howard had a legitimate reason for being there, he's concerned that a black man in this mostly white, upper class neighborhood might not look good discovering a body. So he has to decide if he should split or call the cops. He does the latter. And because of his brief involvement with the now-dead actress he wants to find out what happened to her and why.

I think I wanted to expand beyond the Bunker Hill and Carroll Avenue neighborhoods and Whitley Heights is another old Los Angeles neighborhood that has always fascinated me—Rudolph Valentino and other big stars have lived there throughout the years. And tying in the old Hollywood meets new Hollywood was fun. I also liked setting a scene at the studio backlot. Backlots are another old Hollywood/old Los Angeles thing that I truly love and am fascinated by. I love being on backlots, whether

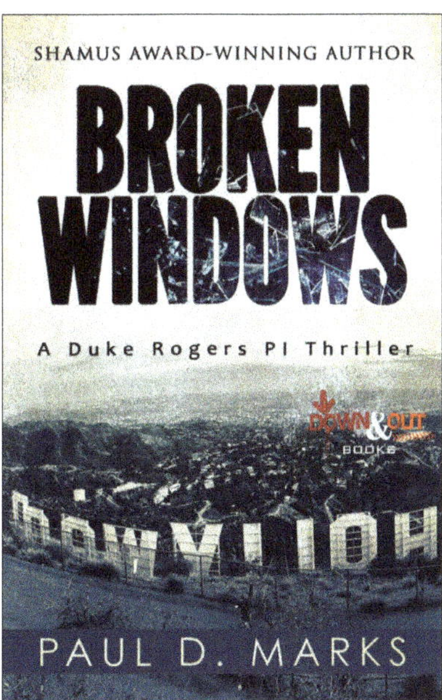

Broken Windows Down & Out Books, 2018

or not filming is happening on them. And I guess you can tell that I love the theme of comparing old to new, especially by including the remaking of a classic old movie.

Ultimately, I look on Los Angeles as its own separate character in the things I write that are set here. And I try to give it a distinct personality. Novelist S.W. Lauden said of one of my works, "I loved how the action bounced around Southern California, almost as if the region was one of the main characters." But wherever I set something I want that location to be its own character.

TDE: What other stories and novels have you written?

PDM: The novels are easier 'cause there's only three published ones. *White Heat*, which won the Shamus Award, introduces private detective Duke Rogers and his very politically incorrect sidekick Jack Riggs. The Duke Rogers series is set

Vortex Timeless Skies Publishing, 2015

during the 1990s in L.A. *White Heat* takes place during the Rodney King riots. Duke inadvertently leads a killer to his prey when he takes on a case to find someone's old high school friend. But it turns out the person he finds is an up and coming young actress and his client ends up murdering her. Now Duke has to make things right and find her killer. *Broken Windows*, the sequel, is set a few years later during the controversial Prop 187 era, where Duke and Jack help investigate the death of an undocumented worker. And *Vortex* is a stand-alone: Zach Tanner is a soldier returning from Afghanistan, who finds it

Bunker Hill Series

- [ ] "Ghosts of Bunker Hill" *EQMM* Dec. 2016
- [ ] "Bunker Hill Blues" *EQMM* Sep/Oct 2017
- [ ] "Fade-Out on Bunker Hill" *EQMM* Mar/Apr 2019

more dangerous here than there.

Five of my previously published stories are collected in the *L.A. Late @ Night* anthology, that can be found at Amazon and other places. And several stories appear in *Ellery Queen*, *Alfred Hitchcock* and other places.

I've also got a new novel coming out in 2020—*The Blues Don't Care*. This one is a little different. It's set on the Los Angeles homefront during World War II, and my detective is a white piano player who plays with an all-black swing band at the famous Club Alabam in Los Angeles. And, of course, there's murder involved. And there's another Duke Rogers novel in the offing that deals with another hot issue of today through the prism of something that actually happened in the 1990s.

TDE: What's the best way to stay current on your upcoming projects?

PDM: People can find out more about me than they'll ever want to know at my website: <PaulDMarks.com> where they can also sign up for my newsletter. I'm also on Facebook, where I talk about L.A., noir, my dogs and things that I find funny or absurd. And I'm on Twitter (@PaulDMarks) and Instagram (PaulDMarks), though I haven't really kicked in on the latter yet. And, as you say, I'm on <SleuthSayers.org> once to twice a month on Tuesdays and every other Friday at <7CriminalMinds.blogspot.com>. I'm all over the place.

And thank you for having me. It's been a blast.

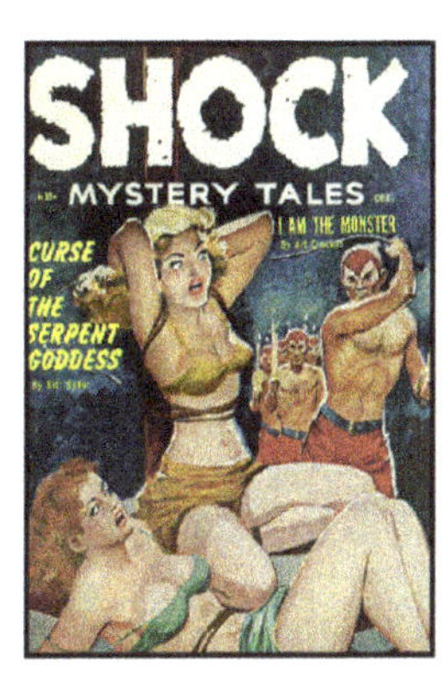

MODERN AGE BOOKS

The finest in vintage pulp fiction for collectors

digests, paperbacks, pulps, & magazines

new catalogs issued monthly

Please call or write for latest catalog

(517) 351-1932 mabooks@comcast.net

PO Box 325, East Lansing, MI 48826

Leo Margulies: Giant of the Digests

Article by Richard Krauss

"The most well-known editor of this era was Leo Margulies, editor-in-chief of more than 70 publications. During the 1930s through the 1940s, he was the highest-paid and probably the best-known pulp magazine editor in the country. He was editor-in-chief of Standard Magazines, known also as Thrilling Publications or The Thrilling Group. During one period, he bought two million words a month.".
–From Philip Sherman's website <leomargulies.com>

Leo Margulies (1900–1975) was the uncle of Philip Sherman, who wrote a biography of the renowned editor and publisher. Sherman's research and personal recollections of Margulies reveal a generous man with an undeniable enthusiasm for fiction and writing. When he was offered his first job, at the tender age of 18, by Robert Hobart Davis (1869–1942), editorial director for *Munsey's Magazine*, he never forgot his mentor who gave him his start in publishing. Years later at Renown Publications, Margulies used the house name Robert Hart Davis to honor his former boss. Behind the Davis pseudonym were authors like Dennis Lynds, Harry Whittington, John W. Jakes, Talmage Powell, I.G. Edwards, Frank Belknap Long, Bill Pronzini, and others who wrote the lead stories for the digests *The Man from U.N.C.L.E.* and *Charlie Chan Mystery Magazine*. Margulies felt Robert Hobart Davis was the greatest editor who ever lived.

The young Margulies began his career at *Munsey's* as an errand boy, but soon began reading manuscripts. By his early 20s, he was selling subsidiary rights, the rights to publish work in alternate formats from the original. And before long he headed the Authors' Sales unit, breaking new ground with sales to *Strand Magazine* in London.

Late in the 1920s, Davis started a literary agency sponsored by the Munsey corporation: Service for Authors. He brought Margulies with him. Within a year or two, internal disputes with the editorial staff flared, and Davis "mostly retired," retaining only partial involvement until 1924, the year Margulies left to work for the Fox Film Corporation, where he stayed for five years.

In 1928, the Woolworth Corporation decided to leverage their network of stores for distribution and began the Tower Magazine line. Catherine A. McNelis, president and publisher of the new venture, hired Margulies to source material and assist in editing tasks for *The Home Magazine*, *The Illustrated Love Magazine*, *The Mystery Magazine*, etc. Initially, the line met with great success, but within five years Tower Magazine was falling apart, at least partly due to the death of McNelis' partner Hugh C. Weir. Margulies must have seen the writing on the wall. Before 1935, when the company declared bankruptcy, Margulies had already moved on to form a new literary agency with partner Jacques Chambrun:

Chambrun and Margulies.

Margulies brought his enthusiasm and work ethic to the new firm, but left after just ten months in the fall of 1929. Sherman's research suggests Margulies did all the work while Chambrun didn't. Rather than continue, Margulies returned to Service for Authors as head of the organization. Although he had a staff of six to help him, again his tenure was relatively short. After a little over a year, he left to form his own agency, Author's Agents, Inc.

He hired Cylvia Kleinman (1911?–1984), a young woman in her early twenties, and likely starting her first job fresh out of college. But business was tough. Sherman shares this excerpt from Margulies' letter to Jay J. Kalez (1895–1982): "This market is so goddam bad and agenting is so darn lousy I'm about to give up the ghost . . ." He soon did, but his place in publishing history was about to gel.

In 1928, Ned L. Pines (1905–1990) began Pines Publishing with Marcus Goldsmith (1881–1963). The enterprise would encompass newspapers, comic books, pulp magazines, and later, the burgeoning paperback book market. In 1931, Street & Smith had ended their relationship with distributor American News Company (ANC), creating a distribution opening. ANC encouraged Pines to start a new line of pulp magazines to fill

---

Note: This article is based primarily on the following references and information pulled directly from Leo Margulies' digest magazines. Additional references are listed at the end.

Leo Margulies Giant of the Pulps by Philip Sherman Altus Press, 2017 (referred to as "Sherman")

Science Fiction, Fantasy, and Weird Fiction Magazines edited by Marshall B. Tymn and Mike Ashley, Greenwood Press, 1985 (referred to as "Tymn/Ashley")

Mystery Book Magazine No. 1 July 1945

the void. Pines hired his friend Leo Margulies as editorial chief over his new line of ten-cent titles: *Thrilling Detective*, *Thrilling Love*, and *Thrilling Adventure*, capitalizing on the leading genres of the day.

Up to this point Margulies had moved with relative frequency from one firm to another learning the ins-and-outs of the publishing business. His network of publishers, agents, and writers was always expanding and second to none. At the Thrilling Group (formally Standard Magazines), he got what he wanted—a top position in a growing company. Pines was the head of the operation, but Margulies is credited with growing the company into one of the leading publishing houses of its era. Part of this success was Margulies

convincing Pines to pay authors on acceptance. He knew Thrilling wasn't necessary the most lucrative market, but since most publishers paid on publication, it gave Thrilling a key competitive advantage. Writers who needed cash quickly, came to where they could get it.

Margulies again hired Cylvia Kleinman to help—this time as an editorial assistant on *Thrilling Love*. Theirs was more than a business relationship; they married on December 27, 1937, and continued working together until Margulies' death in 1975. Kleinman served as Managing Editor on many of the digest magazines Margulies published during the second half of his career. Sherman credits Kleinman as a stabilizing force that helped Margulies maintain his 18-year career with Thrilling.

By 1937, Pines and Margulies had published 25 new pulp magazines, appealing to fans of detective, adventure, romance, sports, western, g-men, fantasy, and science fiction. When they ran out of "Thrilling" titles, they expanded the roster with the illustratives "Exciting" and "Popular," as in *Exciting Baseball*, *Exciting Detective*, *Popular Western*, *Popular Love*, etc. Leveraging the success of hero pulps like Street & Smith's *The Shadow*, Margulies launched *Phantom Detective*, *Captain Future*, and *Hopalong Cassidy's Western Magazine*.

By 1938, Margulies was earning $250 a week, compared to the

Mystery Book Magazine 34 issues
1945 J F M A M J J A S O N D **1946** J F M A M J J A S O N D

Monthly

standard $50 or $75 a week most of his contemporaries earned. In December of that year, Earl Wilson named him "The Little Giant of the Pulps" for his profile in *Writer's Digest*, where he was often cited for his expertise on writing markets.

Coincident with pulp's heyday, was the rise of paperback books. Both offered inexpensive access to a mass audience hungry for reading material of all types. Penguin Books is credited as the first paperback publisher. Their innovative new format crossed the ocean from England in short order. In 1942, Pines and Margulies launched Popular Library which would eventually publish well over 1,000 different titles, many in the crime and western genres.

Mystery Book Magazine

The first, or at least one of the first digest magazines edited by Margulies, *Mystery Book Magazine* was introduced in July 1945. Over the next five years it was published under three different companies (William H. Wise, Mystery Club, and Best Publications), all under the Standard Magazines umbrella. It was not the first nor the last time a publisher attempted to join the concepts of a book and a magazine. Margulies' idea was to publish full-length novels in the magazine that could later be reprinted as paperbacks by Popular Library.

Unlike Standard's pulp magazines, *Mystery Book*'s covers featured minimal artwork, relying on its story

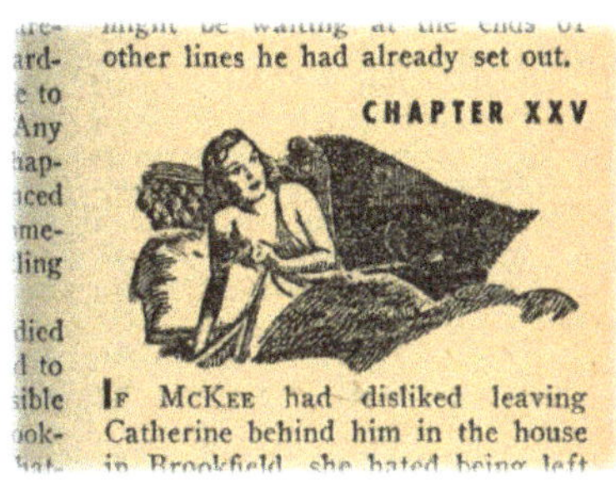

titles and author's names to drive sales. Its authors were often leaders in the mystery field. For example, the first issue featured two new short novels, "Murder is My Business" by Brett Halliday (1904–1977) and "The Spitting Tongue" by Dorothy B. Hughes (1904–1993). *Mystery Book* was intended to compete head-on with the five-year-old *Ellery Queen Mystery Magazine*, which also strove to deliver "The Best in New Crime Fiction," as *Mystery Book*'s slogan proclaimed. Its contents was rounded out with short stories, puzzles, and book reviews by Will Cuppy (1884–1949).

In the opening editorial, Margulies describes his intent:

Mystery Book does not propose to span at one full swoop the vast range of interests, prejudices and fanaticisms that comprise modern detective fiction. It is our intent to publish only new and original stories by the great masters of mystery now writing—no matter whether we put out a magazine containing a dozen

Mystery Book Magazine

1947	J	F	M	A	M	J	Fall	Win	1948	Spg	Sum	Fall	Win
	☐	☐	☐			☐	☐	☐		☐	☐	☐	☐

Bimonthly

Quarterly
Pulp format

Mystery Book Magazine No. 9 March 1946

short stories or one containing but a single full-length novel.

No art director is credited, but the magazine's interior artwork was outstanding. Every story was profusely illustrated with a beautifully detailed splash page and small spot illustrations throughout. In the case of novels, each chapter began with one, so they totaled more than two dozen per issue—simply charming! Unfortunately, the page gutters on the binding edge were poorly configured, making the inside columns difficult to read. I have only six of the digest issues, but the problem is present in all six.

Initially a monthly, the magazine's sales never matched its quality, or ambitions. It went bi-monthly after 16 issues, and quarterly after

19. Its quarterly debut in Fall 1947, was barely recognizable. It expanded to pulp magazine-size and featured the sort of good-girl-art covers common to detective pulps of its era. Its final two issues in Fall 1950 and Winter 1951 changed its name to *Giant Detective*. But by then Margulies had left Standard Publications, ending his 18-year run in 1950.

A bit ironically, Mercury Publications (*Ellery Queen Mystery Magazine*) introduced their own *Mercury Mystery Book-Magazine* in September 1955, which ran for 23 issues through April 1959, dropping "Book" from its title for its final six editions.

Popular Library

Always busy editing magazines for Standard, Margulies somehow found time to create four anthologies for Hampton Publishing (another Standard Publications imprint), two for Popular Library and six published under the Standard Magazines brand.

The Decline of the Pulps

Twice during World War II Margulies served as a war correspondent for Standard Magazines. Apparently, he wanted a first hand look at the war to ensure Standard's wartime magazine stories were authentic. His first deployment was with the Navy where he served in Okinawa in 1943. His length of service is unclear, but he returned in 1945 just prior to the end of the war. On September

Mystery Book Magazine

1949	Spg	Sum	Fall	Win	1950	Spg	Sum	Fall	Win
	☐	☐	☐	☐		☐	☐	☐	☐

Title change:
Giant Detective

2, 1945, Margulies was aboard the *USS Missouri* battleship to witness the formal surrender of Japan on the deck of the ship in Tokyo Bay.

The war had created paper shortages for publishers, contributing to the decline of pulp magazines. By 1945, even the top-selling titles were losing circulation. Thrilling fared better than most, but even they were feeling the effect of the post-war recession. On April 8, 1949 Street & Smith announced the end of their pulp magazine line that included such stalwarts as *The Shadow*, *Doc Savage*, *Detective Story Magazine*, and *Western Story Magazine*. Thrilling discontinued eleven titles between 1950 and 1951, with more coming. The pulps were under threat from multiple sides. Comic books were pulling young readers away. Television was competing for all ages and created a new market for writers. And writers were attracted to the paperback book market as well. It was clear pulp publishing was fighting a losing battle.

In 1950, Margulies and Kleinman took a leave of absence from Standard Magazine to live in France. It wasn't entirely a vacation. Margulies began the process of securing a publisher for a series of anthologies by Leslie Charteris, author of The Saint. He had Charteris' agreement and wanted to sell the series to French publisher Librairie Athéme Fayard through Jenny Bradley of the Bradley Literary Agency. But they weren't convinced it would sell. Ne-

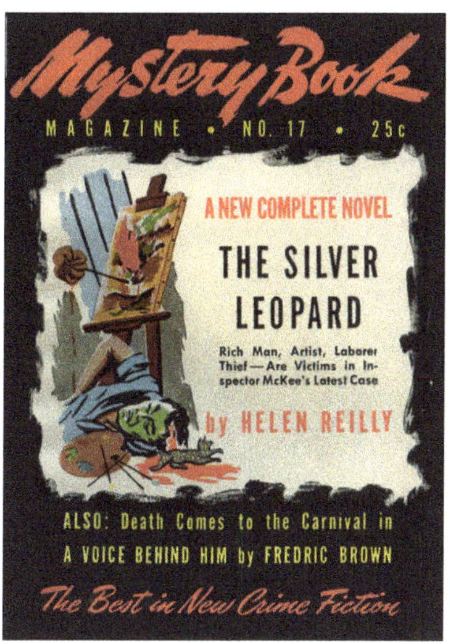

Mystery Book Magazine No. 17 Jan.1947

gotiations were slow and protracted.

Margulies and Kleinman extended their stay in France by three months. Ned Pines could not have been happy. When the couple finally returned to New York in March 1951, Margulies was already making plans to return to France. He parted company with Standard shortly thereafter, whether fired or resigning—or by mutual agreement—is unclear.

Back in France by August, Margulies continued to pitch The Saint anthologies to Fayard through Bradley, but eventually turned to London to source an alternative publisher. He finally struck a deal with Hodder & Stoughton in the United Kingdom and The Crime Club in the United States, so the

Mystery Book Magazine

1951	Spg	Sum	Fall	Win
	☐			

Final issue

series saw print at last. Although Margulies had made all the arrangements, Charteris was credited as editor in all nine titles in the series.

The Saint Detective Magazine

Initially, Margulies had offered *The Saint* magazine to Fayard, but they weren't at all interested. They were publishers of books not magazines. Their reaction had set Margulies on the path to pursue anthologies instead. He and Kleinman would have liked nothing better than to live in France working on a Saint magazine. Instead, he returned to New York and developed two new magazines: *The Saint Detective Magazine* and *Fantastic Universe*. In his post-pulp career Margulies knew his chances for success were better with existing properties. In today's parlance, he wanted properties with platforms. Like Ellery Queen, The Saint was a natural.

Ellery Queen Mystery Magazine was both an inspiration for success and a direct competitor. It was obviously on Leslie Charteris' mind, when he wrote this friendly jibe in his introduction for the second issue of *The Saint* (June-July 1953):

I have a very personal gloat in this issue. For many years Ellery Queen (to use the name under which two good friends prefer to be jointly known) has frequently delved into my lurid past to reprint a Saint story in his own magazine. Until now Ellery Queen had a magazine and I didn't. But now that I'm offering competition it is fun to come up with an Ellery Queen story—TREASURE HUNT.

Margulies joined forces with H. Lawrence Herbert in 1952, and King-Size Publications was formed, with Herbert acting as President, and Margulies as publisher. He hired

The Saint Detective Magazine 141 issues

1953	Spg		J/J	A/S	O/N
☐			☐	☐	☐

Editor: Sam Merwin — Quarterly — Bimonthly

1954	J	F	M	A	M	J	J	A	S	O	N	D
	☐		☐		☐		☐		☐	☐	☐☐

Editor: Beatrice Jones — Editorial Director: Leo Margulies — Monthly

Fantastic Universe 69 issues

1953			J/J	A/S	O/N
			☐	☐	☐

Editor: Sam Merwin, Jr. — Bimonthly

1954	J	F	M	A	M	J	J	A	S	O	N	D
	☐		☐		☐		☐		☐	☐	☐☐

Editor: Beatrice Jones — Editor: Leo Margulies — Monthly

The Saint Detective Magazine Vol. 1 No. 2 June-July 1953

Fantastic Universe Vol. 1 No. 6 May 1954 Cover by Clarence Doore

Sam Merwin, Jr. (1910–1996) as editor for the first year of publication, 1953 (four issues). Merwin was replaced by Beatrice Jones in early 1954 (two issues), and then Margulies himself took over as editor from May 1954 thru July 1956 (25 issues).

In his introduction to the magazine, on the back cover of the first issue (Spring 1953) Margulies wrote:

> *To my way of thinking* The Saint Detective Story Magazine *is a natural. Certainly there is no more widely known and beloved character in present-day mystery fiction than Simon Templar, alias the Saint. And certainly there is no man alive more uniquely equipped to serve in a supervisory capacity on a mystery magazine than Simon's creator."*

Unlike Margulies' later titles where ghost writers sat in for the author of the lead feature, for *The*

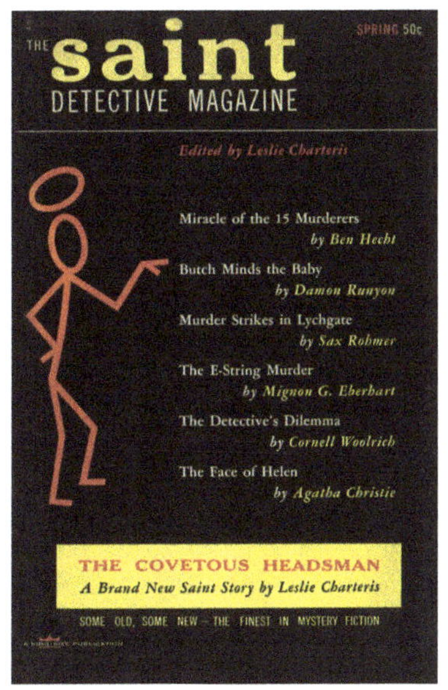

The Saint Detective Magazine Vol. 1 No. 1 Spring 1953

Saint Leslie Charteris himself wrote a new adventure for every issue—at least for a while. He later substituted

The Saint Detective Magazine

1955	J	F	M	A	M	J	J	A	S	O	N	D
	☐	☐	☐	☐	☐	☐	☐	☐	☐	☐	☐	☐

1956	J	F	M	A	M	J	J	A	S	O	N	D
	☐	☐	☐	☐	☐	☐	☐	☐	☐	☐	☐☐	

Margulies' final issue   Editorial Director: Hans Stefan Santesson

Fantastic Universe

1955	J	F	M	A	M	J	J	A	S	O	N	D
	☐	☐	☐	☐	☐	☐	☐	☐	☐	☐	☐	☐

1956	J	F	M	A	M	J	J	A	S	O	N	D
	☐	☐	☐	☐	☐	☐	☐	☐	☐	☐	☐☐	

Margulies' final issue   Editor: Hans Stefan Santesson

Fantastic Universe Vol. 4 No. 1 August 1955 Cover by Kelly Freas

Michael Shayne Mystery Magazine 337 issues

1956	J	F	M	A	M	J	J	A	S	O	N	D
								☐	☐	☐	☐☐	

Editor: Sam Merwin, Jr. Managing Editor: Cylvia Kleinman   Monthly

Satellite Science Fiction 18 issues

1956	J	F	M	A	M	J	J	A	S	O	N	D
									☐		☐	

Monthly Editor: Sam Merwin, Jr. (two issues) Managing Editor: Cylvia Kleinman a series of features like "Instead of The Saint," "The Saint in Modern Art," "As Others See Us," and reprints of earlier Saint adventures. He also wrote the one-page introductions that appeared on the inside front cover throughout the run.

The early success of *The Saint* in the U.S. did not go unnoticed in France. Bradley wrote in April 1953 that Fayard was at last ready to publish the magazine in French. Margulies was taken unawares. Besides the lead story by Charteris, each issue of the magazine published nine or more short stories by other authors. King-Size had only purchased domestic rights. To publish abroad new rights would have to be established. Eventually, the details were worked out and *The Saint* began its foreign editions.

The covers were decidedly boring, subscribing to the school of "contents covers," with only a stick-figured Saint icon to illustrate them. No matter, the digest was quite successful.

Margulies parted with Herbert and King-Size in 1956. He wrote to Bradley, "The personality clashes and, frankly, the fact that not enough money was being made for two people to earn a living—was the cause of my leaving." He considered buying his partner's interests, but the

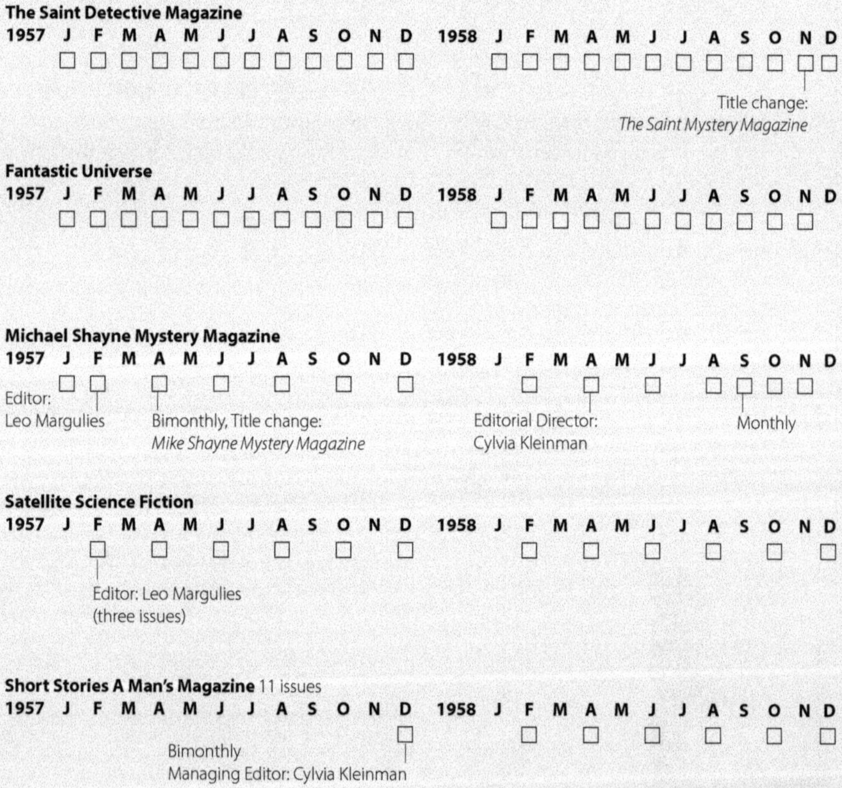

The Saint Detective Magazine

1957   J F M A M J J A S O N D   1958   J F M A M J J A S O N D

Title change:
The Saint Mystery Magazine

Fantastic Universe

1957   J F M A M J J A S O N D   1958   J F M A M J J A S O N D

Michael Shayne Mystery Magazine

1957   J F M A M J J A S O N D   1958   J F M A M J J A S O N D

Editor:
Leo Margulies   Bimonthly, Title change: Editorial Director: Monthly
Mike Shayne Mystery Magazine   Cylvia Kleinman

Satellite Science Fiction

1957   J F M A M J J A S O N D   1958   J F M A M J J A S O N D

Editor: Leo Margulies
(three issues)

Short Stories A Man's Magazine 11 issues

1957   J F M A M J J A S O N D   1958   J F M A M J J A S O N D

Bimonthly
Managing Editor: Cylvia Kleinman

company was heavily in debt, so he decided to sell out his own interests instead. The cash gave him the seed money to start his own line of publications as sole owner. And he didn't lose a moment getting started.

After Margulies left, Hans Stefan Santesson (1914–1975) was made managing editor and remained so until *The Saint* ended in 1967, after 141 issues, over 15 years. The title changed to *The Saint Mystery Magazine* in November 1958 and then simply *The Saint Magazine* as of May 1966. The property was purchased by Great American Publications, noted on the contents page as of October

1959. Leslie Charteris was credited as Supervising Editor throughout the magazine's entire run.

During the first year or so with Great American, the cover design went from the "contents covers" to photography or illustrations, but by the September 1961 issue, they returned to the original style—much to Charteris' liking.

It's surprising *The Saint Magazine* ended in 1967. The popular TV series starring Roger Moore as Simon Templar, which began in 1964, was still going strong through the 1969 season. The series was announced in the October 1963 issue: *But now at long last, he*

The Saint Mystery Magazine
1959 J F M A M J J A S O N D 1960 J F M A M J J A S O N D

Great American

Fantastic Universe
1959 J F M A M J J A S O N D 1960 J F M A M J J A S O N D

Bimonthly Monthly | Pulp format Final issue
Great American

Mike Shayne Mystery Magazine
1959 J F M A M J J A S O N D 1960 J F M A M J J A S O N D

Satellite Science Fiction
1959 J F M A M J J A S O N D

Monthly   Final issue
Bedsheet format
Editorial Director: Cylvia Kleinman

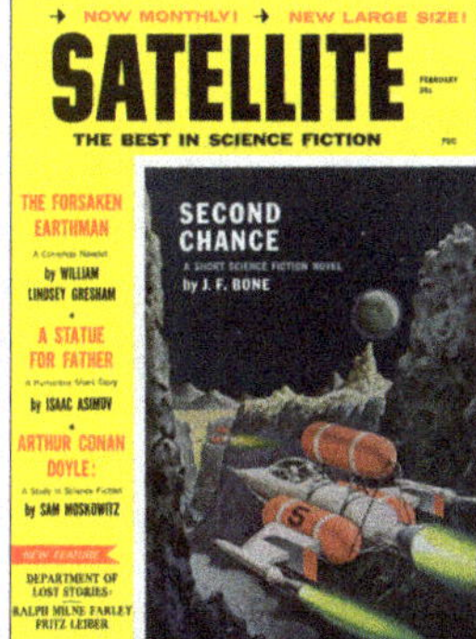

Satellite
Vol. 3 No. 3
Feb. 1959
Cover by
Alex Schomburg

Short Stories A Man's Magazine
1959 J F M A M J J A S O N D

Bedsheet format   Final issue
Title change:
Short Stories For Men

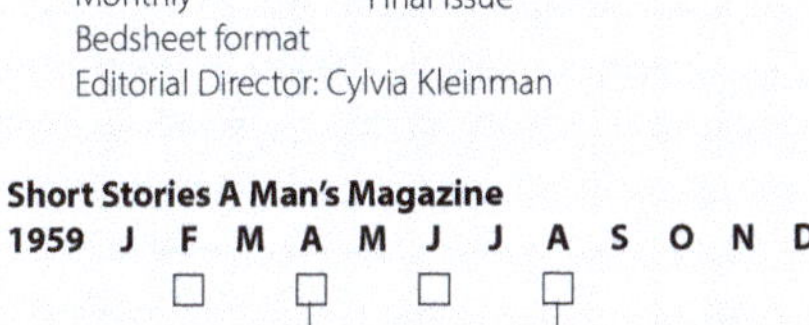

The Saint Mystery Magazine Vol. 19 No. 5
November 1963

The Saint Magazine Vol. 25 No. 6
October 1967 final issue

[Charteris] has agreed to this new ITC series of thirty-nine one-hour productions starring Roger Moore which will be seen beginning this Fall.

The next month (Nov. 1963) Moore himself wrote a three-page synopsis of his delight in landing the role, various objections to him playing the character, and how to best bring the stories to life. Although adaptations, every episode was based on an original story by Charteris. Moore wrote:

The time factor has, of course, been one of our major problems in bringing the Saint stories to television. We have deliberately avoided dating them in any way. They are all given contemporary settings. But in no case have any of the characters changed. Inspector Teal, however, crops up only very infrequently. Only a few of the earlier stories happen to have been selected for the TV series."

The covers of subsequent issues reminded readers to "Watch for the Saint on TV" through April 1966. Thereafter, intermittent promo blurbs moved inside as story-end

The Saint Mystery Magazine

1961 J F M A M J J A S O N D   1962 J F M A M J J A S O N D

Sales Publications   Fiction Publishing

Mike Shayne Mystery Magazine

1961 J F M A M J J A S O N D   1962 J F M A M J J A S O N D space fillers. However, the final four issues of the digest featured scripts from TV episodes adapted by Fleming Lee, with black-and-white photographs from the program front and center on the cover. But this was the end. Financially, the magazine was no longer viable. Santesson took a pay cut to stay on for the final four issues.

Although Charteris knew the final issue would be October 1967, his introduction for the issue never came out with it:

It is no use being bitter about a trend which now seems irreversible. My sadness today comes from remembering how much those old magazines, both "pulp" and "slick", offered me the exercise which any writer, like an athlete, needs to develop himself, and also paid me for learning. There is no such training available to a beginner with limited talent who switches quickly into profitable TV writing, where he only needs to jot a stage direction that "There is an exciting 10-second fight" and leave the rest to the director and the stunt men. And yet, to write the Great Novel which might become a best-selling paperback requires an investment of time spent in possible starvation which might never pay off.

If this insignificant

The Saint Magazine Reader
edited by Leslie Charteris and Hans Santesson
Crime Club, 1966

little Magazine goes down too, at least we tried.

However strong the clues, the subscription solicitation that ran beside the intro was enough red herring to dissuade any doubters. The end came telegraphed only in hindsight.

An Australian edition of *The Saint Detective Magazine*, published by Magazine Enterprises, began in September 1954 and ran until November 1959. The UK edition, also published by Magazine Enterprises in Australia, began in November 1954 and ran until December 1959.

The Saint Mystery Magazine

1963	J	F	M	A	M	J	J	A	S	O	N	D		**1964**	J	F	M	A	M	J	J	A	S	O	N	D
	☐	☐	☐	☐	☐	☐	☐	☐	☐	☐	☐	☐			☐	☐	☐	☐	☐	☐			☐	☐		☐

Mike Shayne Mystery Magazine

1963	J	F	M	A	M	J	J	A	S	O	N	D		**1964**	J	F	M	A	M	J	J	A	S	O	N	D
	☐	☐	☐	☐	☐	☐	☐	☐	☐	☐	☐	☐			☐	☐	☐	☐	☐	☐	☐	☐	☐	☐	☐	☐

Fantastic Universe Vol. 2 No. 2 Sept. 1954

November 1966. Its final eight issues in the UK were as *The Saint Magazine*. And of course, there was finally a French edition. *Le Saint Detective Magazine* began in March 1955 on a monthly schedule and ran until February 1965, when it ended after 120 issues.

Fantastic Universe

The second King-Size title was *Fantastic Universe*. It did not leverage a famous character like The Saint for instant recognition, but science fiction was so popular in the early 1950s Margulies could proceed on the strength of the genre alone. In the introduction from the inaugural issue (June/July 1953) the editors purported there was too much specialization in the field:

It is our intention to give you the greatest possible variety within the entire range of fantasy and science fiction.

Then, Atlas Publishing & Distributing Co. Ltd. took over publishing in the UK, with the title *The Saint Mystery Magazine*, and continued there, from January 1960 through

The Saint Mystery Magazine

1965	J	F	M	A	M	J	J	A	S	O	N	D	1966	J	F	M	A	M	J	J	A	S	O	N	D

Title change: *The Saint Magazine*

Mike Shayne Mystery Magazine

1965	J	F	M	A	M	J	J	A	S	O	N	D	1966	J	F	M	A	M	J	J	A	S	O	N	D

Monthly
Editorial Director: Cylvia Kleinman

Shell Scott Mystery Magazine 9 issues

1966	J	F	M	A	M	J	J	A	S	O	N	D

Bimonthly
Final issue

The Man From U.N.C.L.E. Magazine 24 issues

1966	J	F	M	A	M	J	J	A	S	O	N	D

Monthly
Editorial Director: Cylvia Kleinman

The Girl From U.N.C.L.E. Magazine 7 issues

1966	J	F	M	A	M	J	J	A	S	O	N	D

Bimonthly
Editorial Director: Cylvia Kleinman

The Man From U.N.C.L.E. Vol. 3 No. 2 March 1967

The first issue weighed in at 192 pages and cost 50¢, thicker and more expensive than its newsstand competitors. It was a bold attempt, but as sales figures arrived, the strategy was quickly aligned with the market and the fourth edition proudly proclaimed "Now 35¢" with a revised page count of 160.

The job of editor followed the same path for *Universe* as the previously mentioned *Saint*: Sam Merwin, Jr. (three issues), Beatrice Jones (two issues), and Leo Margulies (26 issues). In October 1955, Hans Stefan Santesson rebooted the book review column, "Universe in Books," which had last appeared in January of that year. When Margulies sold his interest in King-Size in 1956, Santesson took over as Editorial Director for both *Fantastic Universe* (Sept. 1956) and *The Saint* (Aug. 1956).

During the 1950s, the market

Fantastic Universe Vol. 4 No. 2 Sept. 1955

and competition for science fiction digests was thriving. Tymn/Ashley describe *Fantastic Universe* as a middling contender whose success "... must have had some connec-

The Saint Magazine
1967 J F M A M J J A S O N D
Final issue

Mike Shayne Mystery Magazine
1967 J F M A M J J A S O N D   1968 J F M A M J J A S O N D

The Man From U.N.C.L.E. Magazine
1967 J F M A M J J A S O N D   1968 J F M A M J J A S O N D
Final issue

The Girl From U.N.C.L.E. Magazine
1967 J F M A M J J A S O N D
Final issue

The Fantastic Universe Omnibus
edited by Hans Stefan Santesson
Paperback Library 54-633, 1968

tion with its companion magazine, *Saint Detective*, which had proved immensely popular and secured a wide distribution. Distribution was a key factor to survival during the boom period, followed by retail display." Margulies' experience and connections again bore fruit.

If you'd like to read "the best" the magazine had to offer, Prentice-Hall published a hardcover *The Fantastic Universe Omnibus* in 1960 edited by Hans Steffan Santesson. The volume was published in a mass market edition by Paperback Library in 1968.

King-Size eventually sold both properties to Henry Scharf at Great American Publications in 1959, adding the titles to their roster of hot-rod and crossword puzzle magazines. It ended in March 1960 after 69 issues.

Mike Shayne Mystery Magazine

It's unclear exactly when Margulies parted ways with King-Size. His last credits as editor appear in King-Size's late summer 1956 editions. But he must have left earlier because his next two digests debuted barely a month later. If you'll forgive the pun, he was thrilled to be sole owner of his own magazines after a twenty-five-year career working for others.

Margulies had known Davis Dresser, aka Brett Halliday, for years. He published the landmark "Murder is My Business" featuring hardboiled detective Mike Shayne in *Mystery Book Magazine* No. 1 in July 1945. And Halliday remained a regular in that title during Margulies' tenure. *The Saint* and *Fantastic Universe* were proven successes. Margulies followed the same formula when he launched his new company, Renown

Mike Shayne Mystery Magazine
1969 J F M A M J J A S O N D   1970 J F M A M J J A S O N D

Zane Grey Western Magazine 31 issues
1969 J F M A M J J A S O N D   1970 J F M A M J J A S O N D

Monthly
Editorial Director: Cylvia Kleinman

Publications, licensing a popular series character (Shayne) and continuing to mine the popularity of science fiction with *Satellite*.

He described his new detective digest in an August 1956 letter to Jenny Bradley:

Michael Shayne Mystery Magazine [MSMM] is as unlike the Saint Magazine *as day is to night. My magazine is modern and uses no reprints. You will only find brand-new stories in* Michael Shayne, *no reprints ten to twenty years old; no slow-moving, deductive stories. All stories are modern and tough as today's stories should be."*

Like Leslie Charteris, Brett Halliday opened his character's magazine with an introduction, which reads in part:

"It [MSMM] is a project both Leo and I have held in our minds and hearts for many years. But we have waited patiently for the exact moment when the signs were right, when the many and varied elements essential to the production and distribution of a truly fine mystery magazine coincided to make the project feasible."

Unlike Charteris and *The Saint Magazine*, Brett Halliday had little to do with *MSMM*. Sam Merwin,

Michael Shayne Mystery Magazine Vol. 1 No. 4 December 1956

Jr. wrote three of the first four issues' Shayne stories under the Halliday pseudonym. And it's likely he or Margulies wrote the intro pages as well—it wasn't Dresser. Merwin again served as editor for Margulies for the first five issues. When Volume 2 No. 1 (the seventh issue) arrived in April 1957 the title had changed from "Michael" to "Mike," and Margulies was listed as Publisher and Editor, with Cylvia Kleinman as Managing Editor.

Each issue led with a Shayne story ghost written by an impres-

---

Mike Shayne Mystery Magazine

1971	J	F	M	A	M	J	J	A	S	O	N	D	1972	J	F	M	A	M	J	J	A	S	O	N	D
	☐	☐	☐	☐	☐	☐	☐	☐	☐	☐	☐	☐		☐	☐	☐	☐	☐	☐	☐	☐	☐	☐	☐☐	

Zane Grey Western Magazine

1971	J	F M/A	M	J	J	A	S	O	N	D	1972	J	F	M	A	M	J	J	A	S	O	N	D
	☐	☐		☐		☐		☐		☐			☐		☐		☐		☐		☐☐	

Bimonthly   Bedsheet format

Mike Shayne Mystery Magazine Annual 3 issues

1971		Sum		1972		Sum
		☐				☐

Mike Shayne Mystery Magazine Vol. 2 No. 1
April 1957 with Brett Halliday's novel
"Weep for a Blond Corpse" part two

sive roster of crime fiction writers: Sam Merwin, Jr., Robert Terrall, W. Ryerson Johnson, Richard Deming, Robert Arthur, Michael Avallone, Dennis Lynds, Edward Y. Breese, Frank Belknap Long, Max Van Derveer, Bill Pronzini & Jeffrey M. Wallman, David Mazroff, Clayton Matthews & Gary Brandner, George Warren, James M. Reasoner [see interview in *TDE10* June 2019], Livia J. Washburn, Hal Blythe & Charles Sweet, Michael Taylor, and Tim Rourke & James Devlin.

Two of Brett Halliday's novels were serialized for the magazine: *Weep for a Blonde Corpse* (Feb., April, and June 1957) and *The Body That Came Back* (Dec. 1963, Jan. and Feb. 1964)

Shayne was the most successful of Margulies' digests, and one of the

Mike Shayne Mystery Magazine

1973	J	F	M	A	M	J	J	A	S	O	N	D	1974	J	F	M	A	M	J	J	A	S	O	N	D
	□	□	□	□	□	□	□	□	□	□	□	□		□	□	□	□	□	□	□	□	□	□		□

Editor: Thom Montgomery (April 1974)
Managing Editor: Cylvia Kleinman

Zane Grey Western Magazine

1973	J	F	M	A	M	J	J	A	S	O	N	D	1974	J	F	M	A	M	J	J	A	S	O	N	D
	□			□					□								□					□			

Frequency varies (first box) · Final issue (last box, 1974)

Mike Shayne Mystery Magazine Annual

1973	Sum
	□

Final issue

Weird Tales 4 issues

1973	Spg	Sum	Fall	Win	1974	Spg	Sum	Fall	Win
		□	□	□		□			

Quarterly, Pulp format
Editor: Sam Moskowitz
Managing Editor: Cylvia Kleinman
Final issue (Spg 1974)

Charlie Chan Mystery Magazine 4 issues

1973	J	F	M	A	M	J	J	A	S	O	N	D	1974	J	F	M	A	M	J	J	A	S	O	N	D
											□				□		□					□			

Quarterly
Editorial Director: Cylvia Kleinman
Editor: Thom Montgomery
Final issue

most successful digest magazines ever. It ran for 337 issues, mostly monthly, with a few exceptions, from 1956 to 1985. In the early 1970s, there were three annuals (1971–1973). Each included a new Mike Shayne novella and fifteen or more short story reprints, mostly from Renown's *U.N.C.L.E.* titles.

Over its 30-year run *MSMM*'s editors included Sam Merwin, Jr., Frank Belknap Long, William Scott, H.N. Alden, Holmes Taylor, and Thom Montgomery.

Although Leo Margulies died on Dec. 26, 1975, *MSMM*'s masthead continued to list him as Publisher through the July 1976 issue. In August 1976 his title was changed to Founder, Cylvia Kleinman was listed as Managing Editor (then Publisher in Sept. 1976), and Sam

Mike Shayne Mystery Magazine Vol. 18 No. 3 February 1966 with an excerpt of "The Howling Teenagers Affair" from *The Man From U.N.C.L.E.* Vol. 1 No. 1 February 1966

Mike Shayne Mystery Magazine
1975 J F M A M J J A S O N D   **1976** J F M A M J J A S O N D
☐ ☐ ☐ ☐ ☐ ☐ ☐ ☐ ☐ ☐ ☐ ☐   ☐ ☐ ☐ ☐ ☐ ☐ ☐ ☐ ☐ ☐ ☐ ☐

Thom Montgomery's final issue

Editor: Sam Merwin, Jr.

Founder: Leo Margulies

Publisher: Cylvia Kleinman

Mike Shayne Mystery Magazine Annual No. 1 Summer 1971

Mike Shayne Mystery Magazine Vol. 39 No. 6 December 1976

Mike Shayne Mystery Magazine Vol. 39 No. 1
July 1976 Sam Merwin, Jr. returns as editor

Mike Shayne Mystery Magazine Vol. 1 No. 5
May 1957 British Empire Edition

Merwin, Jr. as Editor. Merwin stayed on through August 1979, followed by Larry Shaw (Sept. & Oct 1979); and then Charles E. Fritch, who remained editor until the title ended.

Kleinman sold Renown to Edward and Anita Goldstein in April 1978. Their names replaced Kleinman's on the masthead as Publishers.

Distribution of *The Saint* and *Fantastic Universe* was handled by ANC (American News Company), a monopoly that spun off numerous purportedly independent distributors. One of them, PDC (Publishers Distributing Corporation), handled the distribution for all of Margulies' new titles until May 1969. With the June 1969 issue of *Mike Shayne* the familiar PDC initials were replaced with the King logo, which then appeared on all subsequent Margulies titles.

An Australian edition of *MSMM*, published by Frew Publications and edited by James Grant, reprinted stories from the U.S. edition, other sources, and some original content. The digest began in January 1957 and ran until May/Jun 1958, starting as a 128-page monthly and downsizing to a 112-page bimonthly before it ended its 14-issue run. With only minor differences from the initial dozen issues of the Australian run, the UK version of *MSMM* began in May 1957 and ran until May/ Jun 1958 (12 issues). It rebooted in March 1964 and ran monthly for eight more issues until October 1964, bringing its total to 20 issues.

Satellite Science Fiction

Launched a few months after *MSMM*, *Satellite Science Fiction* debuted with its October 1956 issue. As with *Fantastic Universe*, Margulies anchored his new digest with novels. In his introduction he wrote:

You may ask yourself why another science fiction magazine in a field already so ably filled. The answer, of course, lies in the fact that no magazine today is publishing a complete novel in every issue. The best sft writing is in the book lengths, and installment printing is not entirely satisfactory.

Margulies also planned to print these novels as books, under the imprint Renown Books, opening multiple revenue streams, but the plan created conflict with his distributor PDC, which eventually led to the loss of both *Satellite* and his revival of the long-running *Short Stories* magazine.

The first *Satellite* led with Algis Budrys' novel, "The Man from Earth," which took 84 (66%) of the digest's 128 pages. The balance was filled with short stories by Isaac Asimov, L. Sprague de Camp, Arthur C. Clarke, Craig Rice, Dal Stevens, and Philip K. Dick—who was the author of the

Satellite Science Fiction Vol. 1 No. 1 October 1956

novel featured in the next issue, "A Glass of Darkness." Both of these first two novels did follow with publication in paperback, but not by Renown. After revision, Ace published Dick's novel as *The Cosmic Puppets* in 1957, and Ballantine, Budrys' as *Man of Earth* in 1958.

As it turned out Budrys and Dick were tough acts to follow and sourcing top-quality novels for a magazine may have been more difficult than Margulies had expected. Even many of the back-up stories were mediocre—nothing that threatened *Galaxy* or *F&SF*. Still, *Satellite* had a respectable run of 18 issues. Its innovations include Sam Moskowitz' non-fiction series on science fiction concepts, later

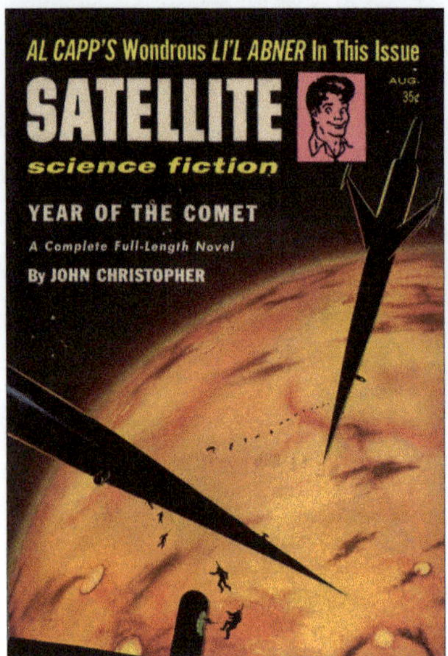

Satellite Science Fiction Vol. 1 No. 6
August 1957

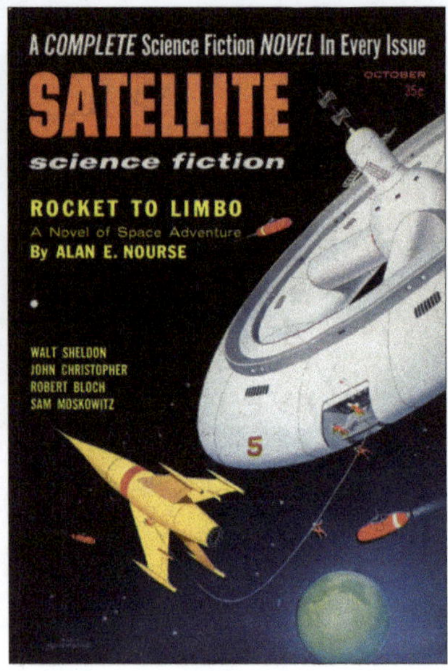

Satellite Science Fiction Vol. 2 No. 1
October 1957

collected and expanded for his book *Explorers of the Infinite* (Cleveland World, 1963), and running the *Li'l Abner* comic strip story, "The Time Capsule," by Al Capp (August 1957).

Among its notable novels were reprints from the UK, reaching the American market for the first time in *Satellite*. These include "The Year of the Comet" by John Christopher (August 1957), "Wall of Fire" by Charles Eric Maine (June 1958), "The Resurrected Man" by E.D. Tubb (December 1958), and "The Man of Absolute Motion" by Noel Loomis (October 1958). The novel most often cited as the best of its run, was Jack Vance's "The Languages of Pao" (December 1957).

The covers of *Satellite* are unique in that they are almost entirely paintings of space craft in outer space rendered by many of the best artists of its era: Ed Emshwiller, Alex Schomburg, Mel Hunter, Robert Braun, Frank R. Paul, and a few others. In the October 1957 issue, Margulies wrote:

We asked Mr. Schomberg to depict a Space Station—a manned Earth satellite—in full color and with depth and breadth and height to it, with the vibrant feel of reality—a Space Station so convincingly three-dimensional that you pass from the airlock of a cruising spaceship to its deck and be welcomed by the Commander with a simple, earnest, friendly greeting, as if you had every right to be there. And we think you'll agree the artist has done just that.

In February 1959, *Satellite* grew from a digest to bedsheet (full-size), intending to make the magazine more noticeable on newsstands. It also increased frequency from bimonthly to monthly and went from featuring full-length novels to short novels. With its primary differentiator gone, the other changes weren't enough to sustain it. After four issues the sales figures arrived—the new format was clearly not the success planned. The final issue was May 1959, although a few copies of the galley proofs for the unpublished June issue survive—now a rare collectible for well-funded enthusiasts.

Short Stories

In 1957, Margulies formed a second company, American Short Stories Corporation and purchased the rights to publish the venerable *Short Stories*, one of the earliest and most successful pulp magazines. Its previous publisher was Codel Publishing, who revived the title in 1956 after a two-year hiatus and published five issues through June 1957. Margulies lost no time and brought the next issue to newsstands in December 1957, adding "A Man's Magazine" to its title.

It began its bimonthly run as a digest-sized magazine despite the fact that nearly every other men's adventure magazine was full size. Perhaps Margulies wanted to differentiate his offering from the competition. Its covers displayed action/adventure paintings without the sex and titillation typical of the genre.

Satellite Science Fiction Vol. 3 No. 2 December 1958

But with the April 1959 issue, the title changed to *Short Stories For Men* with "For Men" in prominence, and expanded to a full-size magazine.

As a digest, it went eight issues with 128 pages each for 35¢; as a bedsheet, it went three, with 80 of the larger-sized pages, still at 35¢. After the title's 70-plus-year lifespan, and 1,114 issues, it finally ended with the August 1959 issue. Of all Margulies' later titles this one seems to command the highest prices in today's secondary markets.

There were two foreign editions during this period, both published by Magazine Enterprises of Australia. The Australian *Short Stories* ran monthly for five issues from Apr/May 1958 to September 1958. The UK *Short Stories*

Short Stories Vol. 220 No. 3
June 1958

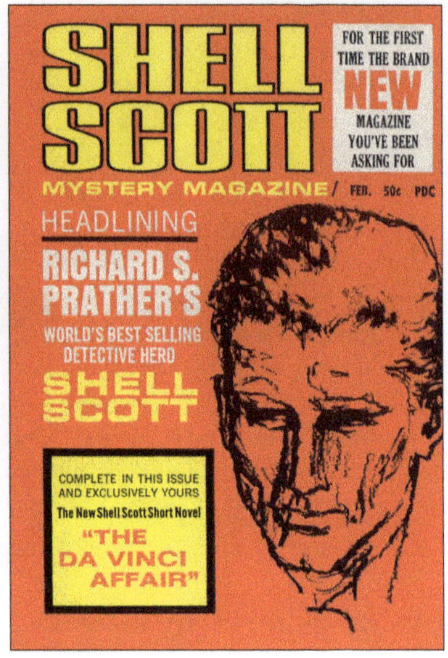

Shell Scott Mystery Magazine Vol. 1 No. 1
February 1966

was a monthly for eight issues from August 1958 to March 1959. Its contents pulled heavily from the U.S. edition, other Renown titles, and a few vintage sources.

Shell Scott Mystery Magazine

Following the success of *Mike Shayne*, Margulies tried for a repeat and launched *Shell Scott Mystery Magazine* in February 1966. Unlike the ghost writers penning Shayne's new adventures, the lead stories in *Shell Scott* were written by his creator, Richard S. Prather (1921–2007). These alternated month to month between new adventures and reprints from *Manhunt, Menace,* and *Cavalier.*

Published by LeMarg Pub-lishing, the digest seemed destined for unqualified success. As noted in the introduction to his first adventure in issue No. 1:

Although Shell Scott, craggy-jawed, hard living private detective, makes his magazine title bow in this issue, he is by no means a stranger to mystery-adventure readers the world over. In fact, more than 40,000,000 copies of his novels have been sold—with tens of thousands pouring off the presses every day!"

Backing up Prather's lead short novel, the magazine filled out its 144 pages with short crime fiction by heavyweights like Donald Westlake, Hal Ellson, James Holding,

Shell Scott Mystery Magazine Vol. 1 No. 4
May 1966

Shell Scott Mystery Magazine Vol. 2 No. 3
November 1966 final issue

Fletcher Flora, John D. MacDonald, Jonathan Craig, Paul W. Fairman, Harry Whittington, Bryce Walton, and others. How could it miss? But, unfortunately it did. Whatever the finances were, they weren't working and Margulies ended the title with the ninth issue in November 1966.

The final issue included Bill Pronzini's first published story, *"You Don't Know What It's Like." Bullets were waiting for me out there in the night, and one had my name on it. I could run, sure. But how far, how long?"*

Margulies served as Publisher on *Shell Scott*, with Kleinman as Editorial Director and H.N. Alden as Associate Editor.

The Man from U.N.C.L.E.

Ian Fleming (1908–1964) and television producer Norman Felton (1913–2012) met late in 1962 to discuss ideas for a new espionage series.

Fleming proposed two characters: Napoleon Solo and April Dancer. Initially, the series was called *Ian Fleming's Solo*. The two exchanged letters discussing the series, but the second James Bond film was in production and Fleming was pressured by producers Albert R. Broccoli and Harry Saltzman to withdraw from the television project. In early 1964, their lawyers demanded Fleming's name be removed from the project as well as the name Solo and Napoleon Solo. The third Bond film, *Goldfinger*, was underway, with Martin Benson playing a supporting role as a character named Mr. Solo.

The parties settled, agreeing the name Napoleon Solo could remain, but the name of the series had to change—thus *The Man From U.N.C.L.E.* was born with Sam Rolfe (1924–1993) as co-creator of the project. Robert Vaughn (1932–2016) was cast as

The Man From U.N.C.L.E. Vol. 1 No. 1
February 1966

The Man From U.N.C.L.E. Vol. 1 No. 1
February 1966 back cover

Solo and David McCallum (1933–) as Illya Kuryakin, replacing April Dancer who later headlined *The Girl From U.N.C.L.E.* spin-off.

The original series first aired on September 22, 1964. It ran for three and a half seasons from 1964 to 1968, canceled midway through season four. Like *Batman* with Adam West, the series skyrocketed to popularity inspiring numerous competitors including *I Spy*, *The Wild Wild West*, and the comedy *Get Smart*, until the public's interest quickly flamed out.

Originally, Rolfe meant to keep the U.N.C.L.E. acronym ambiguous, but MGM's legal department was leery it might be misconstrued as representing the United Nations in a commercial venture, and insisted it be defined. It soon became the United Network Command for Law and Enforcement.

The series' early popularity didn't go unnoticed by Margulies. He soon negotiated rights with MGM for a magazine, and began *The Man From U.N.C.L.E.* digest, published by the Leo Margulies Corporation in February 1966, with financial assistance from PDC (Publishers Distributing Corporation). Each issue led with a "full-length novel" starring Solo, Kuryakin, and their leader, Mr. Waverly written under the house pseudonym Robert Hart Davis. The balance of each issue was filled with short spy and crime stories, and non-fiction features about the television series.

The *U.N.C.L.E.* novels were ghost written by Dennis Lynds, Harry Whittington, John W. Jakes, Talmage Powell, I.G. Edwards, Frank Belknap Long, Richard Curtis, and Bill Pronzini. Part of the agreement with MGM gave the studio approval rights on the novels. They were all originals, not adaptations from the

TV series, to avoid royalty payments to their scriptwriters. The first novel was "The Howling Teenagers Affair" by Dennis Lynds, for which he was paid $450 (the equivalent of $3,550 in 2019). An identical 8-page excerpt from "Teenagers" appeared in the February 1966 issues of *Mike Shayne* and *Shell Scott* to help launch the new magazine.

The next novel, by Harry Whittington, was planned for issue No. 2, but rejected by Frederick Houghton at MGM. It involved the injection of animals with a deadly virus, deemed too similar with Ian Fleming's *On Her Majesty's Secret Service*. Margulies tactfully reminded MGM of the repercussions in a letter, "One story will regrettably have to be scrapped by us—and this means loss of money and the valuable

The Man From U.N.C.L.E. Vol. 4 No. 6 January 1968 final issue

The Man From U.N.C.L.E. Novels
Written as Robert Hart Davis

- [ ] Feb 1966 "The Howling Teenagers Affair" by Dennis Lynds
- [ ] Mar 1966 "The Beauty and Beast Affair" by Harry Whittington
- [ ] Apr 1966 "The Unspeakable Affair" by Dennis Lynds
- [ ] May 1966 "The World's End Affair" by John W. Jakes
- [ ] Jun 1966 "The Vanishing Act Affair" by Dennis Lynds
- [ ] Jul 1966 "The Ghost Riders Affair" by Harry Whittington
- [ ] Aug 1966 "The Cat and Mouse Affair" by Dennis Lynds
- [ ] Sep 1966 "The Brainwash Affair" by Harry Whittington
- [ ] Oct 1966 "The Moby Dick Affair" by John W. Jakes
- [ ] Nov 1966 "The Thrush from THRUSH Affair" by Dennis Lynds
- [ ] Dec 1966 "The Goliath Affair" by John W. Jakes
- [ ] Jan 1967 "The Light-Kill Affair" by Harry Whittington
- [ ] Feb 1967 "The Deadly Dark Affair" by John W. Jakes
- [ ] Mar 1967 "The Hungry World Affair" by Talmage Powell
- [ ] Apr 1967 "The Dolls of Death Affair" by John W. Jakes
- [ ] May 1967 "The Synthetic Storm Affair" by I.G. Edmonds
- [ ] Jun 1967 "The Ugly Man Affair" by John W. Jakes
- [ ] Jul 1967 "The Electronic Frankenstein Affair" by Frank Belknap Long
- [ ] Aug 1967 "The Genghis Khan Affair" by Dennis Lynds
- [ ] Sep 1967 "The Man from Yesterday Affair" by John W. Jakes
- [ ] Oct 1967 "The Mind-Sweeper Affair" by Dennis Lynds
- [ ] Nov 1967 "The Volcano Box Affair" by Richard Curtis
- [ ] Dec 1967 "The Pillars of Salt Affair" by Bill Pronzini
- [ ] Jan 1968 "The Million Monster Affair" by I.G. Edmonds

The Girl From U.N.C.L.E. Vol. 1 No. 1
December 1966

The Girl From U.N.C.L.E. Vol. 1 No. 1
December 1966 back cover

time we so badly need to be on schedule." Fortunately, Whittington banged out a new story in less than two weeks, approval was given, and "The Beauty and Beast Affair" appeared on time in March 1966.

From then on novel outlines were submitted to MGM, and upon approval, the novels were drafted. Meanwhile, Whittington recast his original submission which was eventually published as "The Ship of Horror" in *Mike Shayne* (February 1968).

Each issue of *The Man From U.N.C.L.E.* featured a black-and-white photo of Solo and Kuryakin against a bright solid color background on the cover and a full-size photo on the back cover. Alexander Waverly joined his agents on the cover in March 1967. Although the first season of the TV series was black-and-white, the balance of its run was broadcast in color.

The digest and TV series both ended abruptly in 1968. As was often the case with digests, the final issue (January 1968) included the standard subscription offer and announced the lead novel "The Vanishing City Affair," slated for the February issue that never appeared. If Margulies was true to form, it was recast for another magazine, but the title must have changed as well, making it difficult to identify.

Leo Margulies and Cylvia Kleinman were listed as Publisher and Editorial Director respectively throughout all 24 issues of *The Man From U.N.C.L.E.* H.N. Alden served as Associate Editor from February thru November 1966, followed by Holmes Taylor from December 1966 thru January 1968.

The Man From U.N.C.L.E. proved the most durable of the spy digests. It shares the bookshelf with only a few other notable companions: *American Agent* (1957) two issues, *Intrigue Magazine* (1965–1966) three issues (including a James Bond story by Ian Fleming reprinted in issue No. 2), and *Espionage Magazine* (1984–1987) 14 issues (see Josh Pachter's recollections of *Espionage* in *TDE7* pages 138–147). And of course, *The Girl From U.N.C.L.E.* (1966–1967) seven issues.

The Girl From U.N.C.L.E.

The success of *The Man From U.N.C.L.E.* paved the way for the spinoff series *The Girl From U.N.C.L.E.* that began on September 13, 1966. During development, MGM approached Margulies to publish a spinoff magazine. He was reluctant, the *Man* digest was not nearly as popular as the television program that spawned it, but he finally agreed, to prevent MGM from going elsewhere.

The Girl From U.N.C.L.E. magazine debuted in December 1966 and ran for seven bimonthly issues, ending in December 1967. Like *Man*, every issue of *Girl* opened with a complete novel starring U.N.C.L.E. agents April Dancer (Stefanie Powers 1942–), Mark Slade (Noel Harrison 1934–2013), and Alexander Waverly (Leo G. Carroll 1886–1972)—with Solo and Kuryakin often helping out. The novels, under the Robert Hart Davis house name, were written by Richard Deming, I.G. Edmonds, and Charles Ventura.

Three other series characters appeared in the digest in the short story backup features: Casimiro Lowry by V.A. Levine (twice), Desiree Fleming by Max Van Derveer (twice), and Mr. Mei Wong by Dan Ross (once). Of the three, Mr. Mei Wong was by far the most prolific,

The Girl From U.N.C.L.E. Vol. 1 No. 6 October 1967

with over two dozen adventures published in *The Saint, Mike Shayne, The Man From U.N.C.L.E.,* and *London Mystery Selection.*

Girl's editorial team mirrored *Man*'s, with H.N. Alden serving as Associate Editor for the first three issues, and Holmes Taylor the final four. Whatever happened to "The Utterly Incomprehensible Affair," the novel, scheduled for

The Girl From U.N.C.L.E. Novels
Written as Robert Hart Davis

- ☐ Dec 1966 "The Sheik of Araby Affair" by Richard Deming
- ☐ Feb 1967 "The Velvet Voice Affair" by Richard Deming
- ☐ Apr 1967 "The Burning Air Affair" by I.G. Edmonds
- ☐ Jun 1967 "The Deadly Drug Affair" by Richard Deming
- ☐ Aug 1967 "The Mesmerizing Mist Affair" by Charles Ventura
- ☐ Oct 1967 "The Stolen Spaceman Affair" by I.G. Edmonds
- ☐ Dec 1967 "The Sinister Satellite Affair" by I.G. Edmonds

Zane Grey Western Magazine Vol. 1 No. 5
February 1970

Zane Grey Western Magazine Vol. 2 No. 1
April 1970

the never-published January 1968 issue, is unknown. The digest along with the TV series ended in 1967.

Zane Grey Western Magazine

In May 1968, Margulies acquired rights to publish *Zane Grey Western Magazine* (*ZGWM*) with Romer Zane Grey. Zane Grey's heirs, Romer and Dr. Loren Grey would act as Advisory Editors. New adventures of Grey's series characters Buck Duane, Arizona Ames, Laramie Nelson, Nevada Jim Lacy, Yaqui, Judkins, Burn Hudnall, Al Slingerland, and Jim Cleve, were penned under Romer Zane Grey's name by Tom Curry, Clayton Matthews, Bill Pronzini and Jeffrey M. Wallmann, and others.

Margulies' *ZGWM* reboot began as a monthly digest in October 1969, fifteen years after the long-running Dell digest ended in January 1954. Margulies published the title through another company Zane Grey Western Magazine, Inc., with Kleinman serving as Editorial Director. Margulies loved westerns but introduced his new title as public interest in the genre was fading. It remained monthly through its first full year of publication, then went bimonthly in March 1971. A few months later, in August 1971, the size expanded to 8.5" x 11," along with the corresponding drop in page count from 128 to 64, typical of the digest-to-bedsheet conversion.

Margulies' introduction explains:

While sales in the smaller sized version of this magazine have been gratifying, its pocket book format, besides being often overlooked and hidden on a newsstand, would not permit the many photos, decorative layouts and varied typefaces which will make this new large format edition a truly outstanding magazine, one in fact fully worthy of

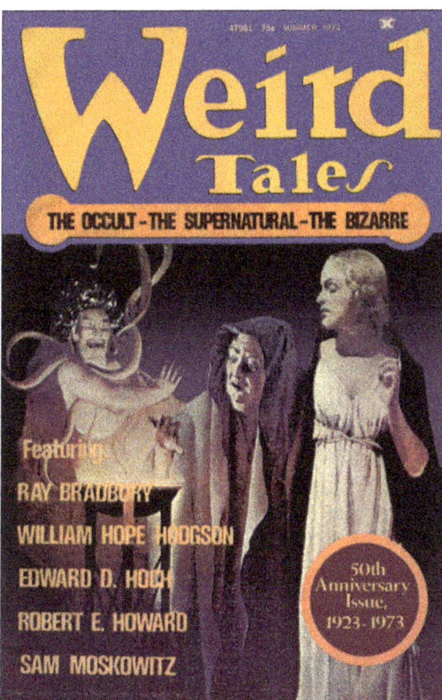

Weird Tales Vol. 47 No. 1 Summer 1973

Weird Tales Vol. 47 No. 3 Winter 1973

the famous name its title bears."

The number of "true west" articles in the new format increased from one per issue to about four. In 1973, the frequency became less predictable and the title ended in September 1974, after 31 issues.

Weird Tales

Margulies' final effort to introduce new titles occurred in 1973. First in Summer, a reboot of the venerable *Weird Tales*, and second, in November 1973, *Charlie Chan Mystery Magazine* (covered in *TDE10* June 2019). Unfortunately, both titles lasted only four issues, about as long as it took for final sales figures to arrive on their debut—so both must have performed poorly.

As early as 1959, Margulies had seriously considered restarting *Weird Tales* (*WT*). He was anxious to publish the magazine, but at the time settled for a series of paperback anthologies: *The Unexpected* (Pyramid G590, 1961), *The Ghoul Keepers* (Pyramid G665, 1961), *Weird Tales* (Pyramid R-1029, 1964), and *Worlds of Weird* (Pyramid R-1125, 1965).

In total, Margulies edited 24 paperback book collections of short stories while on his own, from 1954 through 1967, including a few drawn from his magazines like *Mike Shayne's Torrid Twelve* (Dell K-109, 1961), *Mink is for a Minx* (Dell 5642, 1964), and *The Man From U.N.C.L.E.* (Leo Margulies Corp., 1967*).

With the fiftieth anniversary of *Weird Tales*' founding, Margulies felt the time was right and enlisted the aid of Sam Moskowitz as editor, having worked with him on the two *Weird* paperbacks mentioned earlier. Margulies secured the

*Listed in Sherman's book, but I was unable to find a second source to verify.

Three Times Infinity Gold Medal d1324, 1958

rights to *WT* from Short Stories, Inc. and the contents evolved as Moskowitz explains in his introduction to the Summer 1973 issue:

At first there was the thought of only using reprints from back issues, but this policy really had no future or vitality to it. Too many of the best from Weird Tales *have been anthologized over and over again. The precious few that escaped reprinting are the ones you'll see in our pages. The first issues of the new* Weird Tales *will be composed chiefly from reprint sources so little known and so difficult to find, that for all intents and purposes they could be considered new stories. Superb and neglected works will be presented from the files of the finest magazines of their time, both British and American.*

Foremost among these stories' authors was William Hope Hodgson, whom Moskowitz featured in his article, "The Early Years," in the debut issue.

The magazine was pulp-size (6.25" x 9.375"), published quarterly by "Weird Tales" from an address in Los Angeles, CA, where Margulies and Kleinman had moved from their longtime home in New York, in May 1972. As usual, Margulies was Publisher, and Kleinman was Managing Editor. The final issue was dated Spring 1974.

Since then, *Weird Tales* has changed hands several times, but is still in print today. The current the issue as of this writing, No. 363, was published by John Harlacher and edited by Marvin Kaye.

Wrap-Up

In 1968, there was an effort by Michael Avallone and Polan Banks to secure an Edgar award for Margulies from the Mystery Writers of America. Unfortunately, the effort failed and the lifelong "friend of mystery" did not receive the prestigious Raven Award for his work as an editor, until 1976—posthumously.

Leo Margulies was a giant of the pulps. From his early start with Robert Hobart Davis at *Munsey's*, he learned the publishing and editing business quickly during a secession of jobs at Service for Authors, Fox Films, Tower Magazines, and his partnership with Jacques Chambrun. He rode the wave of pulp publishing's greatest era with Ned Pines at the Thrilling Group for eighteen years. No doubt he was in the right place at the right time, but it was his skill and work ethic that made his reputation.

In some ways his second act was more impressive that his first. After the pulps, competition from other media was greater, and time spent reading was trending down. Yet Margulies made a successful career with digests, when few others could say the same. His business acumen, networking skills, and knowledge of public interest allowed him to continue, launching two of the most successful mystery digests in history: *The Saint* and *Mike Shayne*. And like his earlier days in the pulps, he managed to bring to life magazines that spanned nearly every genre: science fiction, mystery, adventure, espionage, fantasy, and western. He was truly a giant of the digests as well as the pulps.

Additional References
The History of Science Fiction Magazines
    Vol. 2 by Michael Ashley
    Liverpool University Press, 2000
*Mystery, Detective, and Espionage
    Magazines* by Michael L. Cook
    Greenwood Press, 1983
The Man From U.N.C.L.E. Book
    by Jon Heitland Macmillian, 1987
*The Saint: A Complete History in Print,
    Radio, Film and Television of Leslie
    Charteris' Robin Hood of Modern
    Crime, Simon Templar 1928–1992*
    by Burl Barer McFarland, 2003
Websites
Galactic Central
<spycommandfeatures.wordpress.com>
<wikipedia.org>
<lofficier.com/saint.html>

The X-Files Comics Digest

Topps Comics Inc., New York, NY
Three issues
December 1995 to September 1996
5-1/4" x 7-3/8"
$3.50 (No. 1 & 2) $3.95 (No. 3) cover price

The X-Files Comics Digest No. 1 Dec. 1995

Bent Lemons
aging hippie

DIDJA SEE WHAT I JUST SAW?

TIME TO TAKE A BREAK!

A QUICK WALK AROUND THE BLOCK WILL DO ME GOOD

ESPECIALLY ON MY SEGWAY

WHOA!
ZING
ZAP!
POW

YEOW!

ARRRRRR
NO!!

YIPE!
POW

THAT STUFF ALWAYS HAPPENS TO ME WHEN I BINGE READ MY DIGEST MAGAZINES!
COOL!
JOTKO

The Good Soldier

Fantasy fiction by Vince Nowell, Sr.
Collage by Marc Myers

But on this magnificent day of all days so far in his life—hopes on high—Toby went seeking the ultimate.

1.

A sunny day, warmer than expected for March. A good day to be fourteen years old. An even greater day because today Toby was out of school for Easter vacation. And it was an especially great day—a "super" day—because Tobias "Toby" Garland had just received a deer rifle for his birthday.

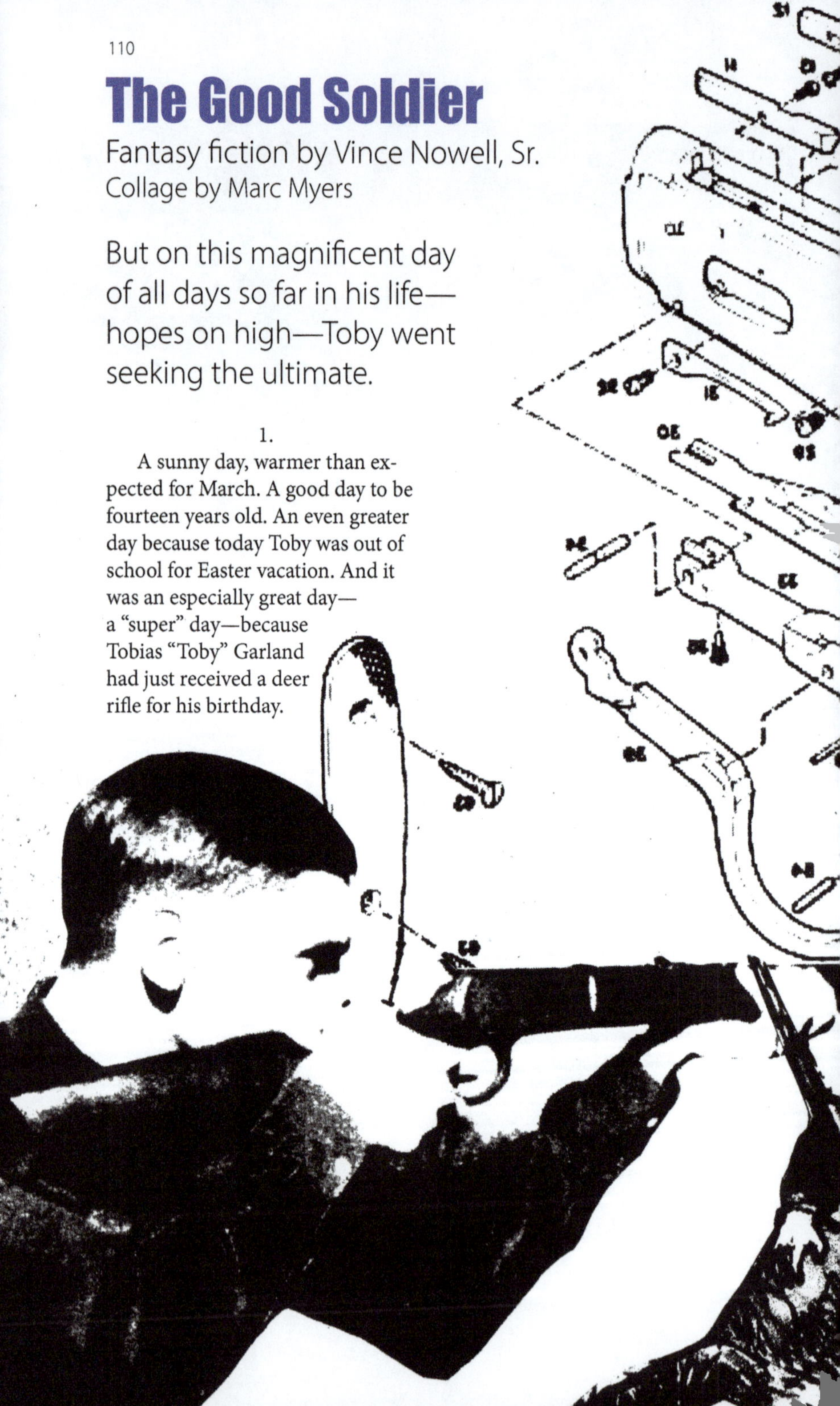

It wasn't truly a "new" rifle because it had long belonged to his Uncle Matthias. It had been his old standby rifle. His "sure-shot piece," as he liked to describe it.

And now it belonged to Toby.

Owning a rifle meant special things to a young man in Hampton County. It meant maturity, first of all—being recognized as a man, no longer as a child. It meant taking on more responsibility. It meant that one had joined that quiet, rarely spoken of group of men who thought themselves to be the steadfast patriots of South Carolina.

So on this sunny day Toby took his "new" Winchester Model 94 lever-action "shootin' 'arn" and went out to find what was available as a sure-enough target. No shooting at mailboxes for him. No squirrel hunting—there'd be little left if he hit one. The same for the small but very fast wild rabbits that ranged through-out Hampton and the adjacent counties of Jasper and Allendale.

No, Toby was ready—or be-lieved he was ready—for big game. Except, of course, that big game was already a scarce commodity in this county that now held less than 18, 000 people in the year 1942.

There had once been a lot more folks around. Now the big war—the Second World War, as it was known in town-talk and in school—was reducing the population, males in particular. Even some of the women were now gone as Army wives or war-workers in some of the big city production plants.

There were no movie houses to distract Toby in this rural area, even if he could have afforded the price of admission. On the rare occa-sions when he traveled the seven or so miles into Fletcher, the nearest town, with his Uncle Matthias, Toby heard his only entertainment coming from a jukebox in Silver's Tavern. He would wait outside while Uncle Matthias went inside to, as he described it, "Check on the tem-pa-chur o' things." While waiting, Toby always hoped to hear his favorite, which his uncle called a "disgusting" song, *Cow-Cow Boogie* belted out in a lusty voice by someone named Ella Mae Morse.

But on this magnificent day of all days so far in his life—hopes on high—Toby went seeking the ultimate. If he could just bring down a deer, he'd be able to provide meat for his uncle and himself for quite a spell.

He imagined what it might feel like to take down a deer. His imagination never extended to the point of foreseeing skinning the carcass, much less carting home any large amount of meat. Such details were beyond Toby's excited imagina-tion on this day. This special day.

But by the time it began grow-ing dark Toby had yet to spot

anything living to shoot at. Knowing he had to scurry home to be in time for supper, he took one quick shot at a distant oak tree. He wasn't sure he even hit it, however. Yet from even farther away came the sound of another gunshot.

An echo? It was almost like a response to his shot. But darkness was gathering and Toby didn't have time to ponder the far-away sound. He headed for home and the supper made by Uncle Matthias, whom the adult men in town called "Matt."

But that was a name for grown-ups to use, not fourteen-year-olds.

2.

Chores. Always repairs and more chores. Uncle Matthias was getting up in years—he was nearly fifty-five now—and needed help around the homestead. He hadn't always had Toby's aid. Toby was sort-of inherited. He was the son of Matthias' youngest (and late-) brother Richard and a woman known as Ruthie. After Richard unexpectedly died young, Ruthie took up with her "good-for-nothin' drinkin' partner" who called himself Ned. Ned and Ruthie ran off when Toby was only seven years old. Within two years Ruthie asked her brother-in-law in a letter to keep Toby permanently when she was close to passing from what Doc' Harver called "alcohol poisoning of the liver."

Matthias' nephew grew to become a treasure, bright and sturdy. He was now nearly five-foot-ten tall. He could read "real good," and had an aptitude for school subjects. Matthias knew that this year would be Toby's last year of schoolin', as attending ninth-grade meant traveling daily all the way to the high school in Garnett. That was a rigorous trip of more than fifteen miles one way—too far to walk every day, and impractical to reach using Matthias' only horse and wagon. Besides, eight years of "learnin'" had been good enough for Matthias, so it would be all right for Toby.

Toby, sandy-haired and tanned from being in the sun a lot, worked at the small family farm for three more days before he had another chance to take his rifle and again strike out for a hunting adventure.

This time he headed west. He knew that if he went far enough he'd end up somewhere near Georgia where the Savannah River established the boundary between the two states. He didn't want to go that far because he'd always been told that Georgia people were ornery and did not abide strangers near their territory. Thus, as he traveled westerly, he also angled gradually northward.

If there was one thing Toby had learned well in the years of school he'd been allowed to attend, it was geography, especially map-reading. Thus he was aware that he was many miles from home as it began getting on toward dusk.

As Toby decided it was time to go back home, strangely, way off ahead, he saw a building. It was tall with columns along one side —a mansion. He thought for sure it looked like pictures he'd seen of old plantation homes. Except that he'd heard there had been no plantations around here for more than a half-century or so.

In spite of the lateness of the day, Toby was tempted to approach closer. He finally realized that what he saw was probably on the Georgia side of the river, and so was impossible to reach. He decided to turn back when he saw a light in a mansion window. It wasn't an electric light, like they had at school. It flickered as would a lantern or a candle. Then it disappeared and Toby turned around to start for home.

As he had done before, he took a parting shot at a distant oak tree. He wasn't even considering that he only had a limited amount of shells and no money of his own to buy more.

As he started to cut through some woods, he again heard a responding gunshot. Except that this time it came from fairly close by and he saw some splinters fly off a tree several feet away to his left.

Scared as hell, he dived into some brush. He wasn't sure if someone had shot back at him, but he wasn't taking any chances. While he hid in the brush, he worried that the beating of his heart could be heard if anyone came by.

And someone did come by.

Through the dimming light of day's end he caught glimpses of three men walking along carefully some forty feet away. They all had rifles. But what was unusual was that all three men wore blue coats, blue pants, and flattop blue hats, something like baseball caps. He recognized their clothing from his readings in school books. They were dressed as Union soldiers from the time of what his uncle and other local men called the "War of Northern Aggression," over seventy years ago. That could not be, Toby thought.

They were too far away for him to consider hailing them.

These fellas, he thought to himself, had to be some rascals from Georgia across the Savannah River pretending to be soldiers.

They were too far away for him to catch more than an occasional word of their conversation. What little he could make out sounded strange. These men spoke with some kind of accent. Yankee? Toby wasn't sure, but he knew it wasn't like the locals sounded.

Toby decided he wanted no truck with them, no matter who they were.

He waited in hiding for what must have been several hours. A waning gibbous moon was well above the night horizon before Toby stirred from his hiding place.

He caught some harsh language from Uncle Matthias when he got home. Toby used the excuse that he had gotten lost, a tale his uncle only reluctantly accepted. Nevertheless, Toby was told to stay close by—except for going to school—for two weeks to pay for his irresponsibility.

Toby worked harder than ever to try to regain his uncle's trust. One day he asked his uncle if he knew of any plantations off toward the west.

Uncle Matthias replied, "Ain't no plantations any more, 'specially 'round heah. Might o' been back eighty years past, but no more."

He also tried to find out more about Union soldiers from the limited library of books at school. He asked his teacher, Miss Diedre, if soldiers from the North had ever come into Hampton County, as well as whether there were any old plantations nearby.

Deidre Brown was one of the three teachers at the Fletcher school. She taught the children who were in the sixth through eighth grades. A graduate of the Technical Col-lege of the Low Country, which had begun as Mather School in 1868, her ambition was to complete her education and earn a full bachelor's degree. However, for now, she had to earn a living.

"Did we have any plantations near here," Toby asked one day in early May.

Miss Diedre responded, "I'm not sure about any plantations nearby. However far out to the west from here, where I was raised on a wheat farm, there was a burnt-out manor house across the river. I imagine it's probably just rubble by now."

She also told Toby, "It isn't beyond belief that Yankee troops may have been in our vicinity during the War Between the States. We've got a fair share of history 'round here."

However, Toby was not satisfied with what he had been told. And he never told his uncle or anyone else what he had seen, or experienced.

3.

Toby didn't have a chance to go on another hunt until after part of the early crop was harvested and hauled into town. When he did get out, he traced his earlier journey west-by-northwest. He had walked a good many miles when he spotted a wild turkey on the ground.

The bird was unusually large—maybe as much as twelve or fourteen pounds, Toby guessed. He stopped absolutely still and watched the bird walk about looking among the grass tufts for bugs or other things to eat. Toby slowly raised his rifle, careful not to move fast or make a sound. Wild turkeys had limited flying ability but could get away into trees quickly if startled. One clean shot to the upper neck took the bird down.

Toby was approaching his

game when a shot flew by closely and struck a tree behind him. "What the hell," he said, using a word he knew to be forbidden. Scared, he crouched down right in front of his dead turkey.

He saw a group of four men moving in his direction. They were dressed strangely in red jackets and soiled white pants. They wore strange hats on the heads. All four had long rifles in their hands.

One of the men raised his weapon and fired at Toby. Fortunately the shot missed him, but the incident infuriated the young man. He raised his rifle and shot at the group without even thinking of the consequences of his action. He was, after all, under attack.

The Winchester proved true to its reputation as an accurate shooting piece. One of the men suddenly clutched at his belly and went down. Toby watched in shock, then stood up. As he did so, another of the red-coated men aimed and shot at Toby.

Toby felt a hard blow to his chest and in wonderment, crumpled to the ground. As he breathed his last, lying on his rifle with one arm over the dead turkey, the men tried to gather up their wounded companion.

"Aye, lads we've gotta get Leonard back to camp. 'e's bleedin' bad," said one of the red-coated men. But Toby was now deaf to their words, as well as any awareness that they turned to go back northward.

The day passed without further incident. It passed without further movement. Or life.

4.

Toby's absence led Uncle Matthias to go into Fletcher to ask for help. Someone called the sheriff who came in from Garnett and a search party was formed. Even with fifty or more men and several good hound dogs, it took two days of searching before they found Toby's body. The double kills were beginning to emit foul smells after the hot days that had passed.

Toby's body was taken to Garnett where they had the medical facilities to do a post-mortem. Everybody in the community for miles around became aware of what had happened. They also found out that Matthias could not afford a decent funeral.

Collections were taken up to assist the Garland family and when the body was ready in a plain wooden coffin, Matthias drove his wagon the fifteen miles to Garnett and brought Toby home to the tiny local cemetery in Fletcher. Because of his and the Garland family's long military background, Matthias had the words "He had the makings of a Good Soldier" inscribed on the headstone.

Matthias spent the next several days grieving while his final crop went unharvested.

On a very hot afternoon a dusty old Ford coup pulled into Matthias' farmyard. Sheriff Evers got out and walked up to the front porch of the Garland farmhouse.

"Hi'ya, Matt," Evers said to the sad-looking man on the porch. "How're ya getting' by?" he asked.

"It ain't easy, sheriff," Matthias answered. "That boy was somethin' special to me. I miss him sorely."

"What brings y'all the way out here, sheriff?" the tired old man asked.

"Couple o' strange things, Matt. One of the searchers looked around the area where Toby was shot.

Some distance away he found a lot of dried blood and this odd-lookin' hat." He offered Matthias a very dusty tricornered hat.

"Don't 'spose it belonged to Toby, but I thought I'd better check," the Sheriff Evers said, thrusting the hat toward Matthias.

"Nope. Ain't Toby's," Matthias answered, handing back the black hat with gold braid around the brim.

"And 'nother odd thing," Evers said. "When the post-mortem was done, we found that Toby had been killed with this, not a bullet."

He held out his palm to reveal a somewhat rounded wad of material.

"What is it," asked Matthias.

"A musket ball," Evers answered. "Somebody said it's the kind of thing they used as ammunition in the War of Independence. But that was more'n a hundred sixty-five years ago."

Matthias didn't say any more. Eventually Sheriff Evers left the porch, got into his Ford, and drove off.

Vince Nowell (Sr.), a sixth-generation native Californian, is a retired technical writer. As the editor of the Operating Manual for the J-2 rocket engine, he was on the project team for the Apollo 11 Moon Landing Program in 1969. His aerospace background encompasses missile instrumentation and test engineering. An avid reader since elementary school, Vince has been reading and collecting science fiction & fantasy since 1950. With a degree in history, a subject he taught in community colleges, he now enjoys researching the history of SF magazines and the backgrounds of authors.

Sword & Sorcery Annual

Published in the Winter of 1974/75, *Sword & Sorcery Annual* was one of Sol Cohen's best reprint books. The issue does double-duty as a "Fantastic Stories Special," although a second issue never appeared.

Cohen acquired reprint rights to Robert E. Howard's "Queen of the Black Coast," which originally saw print in *Weird Tales* May 1934, in order to lead with a Conan adventure. The story was lightly edited by L. Sprague de Camp. The balance of the issue consisted of reprints from Cohen's back files, but new artwork was added—the front and inside front covers, and spot illos for Howard's story, by Steve Fabian.

Sam Moskowitz's profile: "L. Sprague de Camp: Sword and Satire," first appeared in *Amazing Stories* Feb. 1964.

John Jakes' Brak the Barbarian adventure, "The Pillars of Chambalor," first appeared as the cover story in *Fantastic* March 1965. Gray Morrow drew the art for the opening spread.

"Master of Chaos" stars Earl Aubec, by Michael Moorcock, reprinted from *Fantastic* May 1964, along with Virgil Finlay's illustration.

Robert Arthur's "The Mirror of Cagliostro" is an adaptation of his *Thriller* script, "The Prisoner in the Mirror," first broadcast on May 23, 1961, and reprinted from the cover story of *Fantastic* June 1963, with interior artwork by Dan Adkins.

Fritz Leiber's Fafhrd and the Grey Mouser appear in "The Cloud of Hate," from *Fantastic* May 1963, with art by Leo R. Summers.

"The Masters" by Ursula K. Le Guin is reprinted from *Fantastic* Feb. 1963, with art by Dan Adkins.

Roger Zelazny's "Horseman!" reprinted from *Fantastic* August 1962, with art by Leo R. Summers, rounds out the issue.

Sword & Sorcery Winter 1974/75
Ultimate Publishing Co. Flushing, NY
Editor: Sol Cohen
5.25" x 7.75" 128 pages 75¢

References

Galactic Central website
Science Fiction, Fantasy, and Weird Fiction Magazines edited by Marshall B. Tymn and Mike Ashley, Greenwood Press, 1985

FANTASY ILLUSTRATED

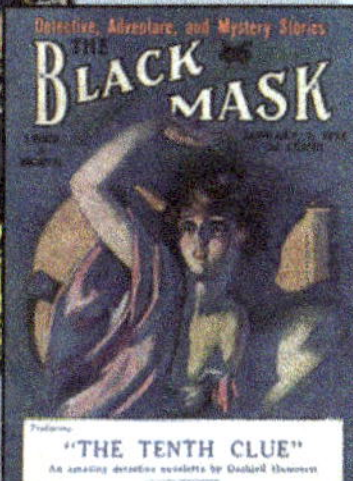

ACTIVELY BUYING

High prices paid. All genres wanted. One piece or lifetime collections. No collection too large or small.

ACTIVELY SELLING

Thousands of Pulps in stock. We love servicing your want lists. Items added to our website weekly.

www.FantasyIllustrated.net

DEALING SINCE 1969

Prompt professional service. Specializing in Pulp magazines and science fiction/fantasy/horror first editions. Vintage paperbacks and comic books.

Contact DAVE SMITH

(425) 750-4513 - (360) 652-0339
rocketbat@msn.com
P.O. Box 248 Silvana, WA   98287

www.FantasyIllustrated.net

Tough 2: Crime Stories

Review by Richard Krauss

Curley looked for prints in the area, moving carefully all around the body now, and out from it in a circle. He had to sit down when he finally saw it, on the other side of the tree.

"With Hair Blacker Than Coal" by Chris McGinley *Tough 2: Crime Stories* August 2019

Itsy Bitsy Spider
by Michael Bracken

In his interview for *TDE8*, Michael Bracken described his character: "Morris Ronald 'Moe Ron' Boyette is a Waco, Texas-based private eye who first appeared in 'Feel the Pain' (*Flesh & Blood: Guilty as Sin*, Mysterious Press, 2003)." With this story for *Tough*, his adventures now number somewhere north of six. Boyette operates out of an office behind Millie's Tattoos and Piercings, run by Millard Wayne Trout, and adjacent to Big Mac's Bail Bonds, run by Lester Beeson.

Boyette is sometimes a bounty-hunter-for-hire for Beeson, tracking down his absentee clients, with an assist from Millie when needed, as in "Itsy Bitsy Spider." But tracking down Carl Weaver is only a subplot, the real mystery is why "Moe Ron" emerges when sexy college girl, Mona Peterson, hires him to clean up the mess she left at her university. Great, hard-boiled fun.

The Third Jump of Frankie Buffalo
by Thomas Pluck

The plan, along with Frankie's role in it, comes clear by the time the half-ton Mack he's driving grinds to a halt while the tracks clear. The engine idles as the journey that brought him here plays out in his head, along with the slow realization that the wheels are about to come off the plan—and that's not the worst of it. Like a mountain snow storm, tense and exhilarating.

Day Planner by Matt Mattilla

A veteran of *Shotgun Honey*, Flash Fiction Offensive, and *Rouge*, Matilla records the crucial minutes of his tale, diary style. You can feel the grit and grime of the homeless milieu, as his mean street kid's unambitious day goes critical.

Tally Ho
by William R. Soldan

Cabbie Gordon Jurewicz is jolted out of his mundane routine by the smile of college-age fare, far too young for him and far too ragged. But Gordon's stilted outlook blinds him to Haley's cloying charms. A bittersweet fantasy ride headed straight to hell. Soldan's work was understandably nominated for Pushcarts twice. His first book was *In Just the Right Light*, a linked short story collection from Unsolicited Press.

Beach Body
by C.A. Rowland

Anne explains why James is a serial philanderer: "My husband has a high sex drive. He'd have sex six times a day if I were willing. I'm not." When the couple finds a body on the beach during their morning walk, the tragedy slowly engulfs their lives. C.A. Rowland's stories appear in *Fiction River* and anthologies like *King of Ages* and *That Hoodoo, Voodoo That You Do*.

Viking Funeral
by Nick Kolakowski

Miller and Alex give Piosa a viking-style sendoff. Alex is half drunk and Miller, appropriate for the occasion, is a real hothead. Piosa's brother is left with nothing but memories. Even darker than Walter and the Dude's sendoff for Donny. Kolakowski's stories have appeared in *Thuglit*, *Crime Syndicate*, *Switchblade*, etc. His most recent novel is *Boise Longpig Hunting Club* from Down & Out Books.

Long Drive Home
by Andrew Welsh-Huggins

Sex, drugs, and violence dog the victims and serve their masters in two separate tales of abuse that unravel in alternating sequence. Each devolves as the pages and players accelerate toward a collision in a Floridian motel room. Great pacing and plotting lead to a satisfying, smart end. Welsh-Huggins' stories have appeared in *Down and Out: The Magazine*, *Mystery Weekly Magazine*, and *Kings River Life*. He is the author of the Andy Hayes mystery series published by Swallow Press.

Masonry
by Rob McClure Smith

Bravado and machismo run amuck when Cowan meets Jalil. Their trash talk turns deadly when Prince Hall joins the scene to uneven the odds. Riveting and brutal. Smith's work appears in a half dozen *Reviews*. *The Violence* is a collection of his shorts published by Queen's Ferry Press in 2015.

Once Upon a Time in Chicago
by Tia J'anae

Frothy tale of two hustlers scratching each other's itch in the backseat of a car until the darkness discovers their rendez-vous. Short, fast, and tough.

The Grass Below My Feet
by S.A. Cosby

The Coldwater Correctional Facility is Turner's home, now and forever. But when his mama dies, he gets a ride over to the funeral home to see her laid out. The past plays out in his mind at the view-ing and conjures an idea. What the hell, he's got nothing to lose, right? Cosby writes fantasy, horror, and crime fiction, and poetry likewise. His story, "Slant-Six," was selected as a Distinguished Story for *Best American Mystery Stories 2016*. His books include *My Darkest Prayer* and *Brotherhood of the Blade*.

No News is Good News
by Evelyn DeShane

The body of a transgender wom-an is found in a ravine. The police think it may be a serial killer. Mar-sha, the woman who discovered the body, has a deeper understanding of trans than most. Her sister is living as a man, saving up for the surgery. And Marsha could be closer to the killer than she thinks. DeShane's creative works have been nominated for The Pushcart Prize, Best of the Net, and for the Sunburst Awards.

The Bag Girl
by Alec Cizak

Two addicts run a scam at the grocery store. She spots a mark at the checkout, getting cash with their purchase, and sends a quick text to her partner, outside. He jumps in from behind and takes off with the cash. It's all good until the cops notice the pattern. Desperate, raw, and brutal. Cizak is the editor of *Pulp Modern*, a filmmaker, author of numerous short stories, an-thologies like *Lake County Incidents*, and novels like *Breaking Glass*.

Sarah, Sweet and Stealthy
by Preston Lang

An engaging hunt by the victim and an unlikely amateur sleuth, for "Samson," a one-night-stand who turned criminal in the early morning hours. Loaded with quirk and verve. Lang is author of the collection *This One is Trouble*, and the novels *Sunk Costs*, *The Sin Tax*, and *The Blind Rooster*.

With Hair Blacker Than Coal
by Chris McGinley

More horror than crime, a pair of poachers mutilate a black bear and head into the deep holler for further profligacy. Sheriff Curley Knott aims to bring them in but mother nature seeks justice in her own way. McGinley teaches middle school in Lexington, Kentucky. His stories have appeared in *Out of the Gutter, Mystery Weekly Magazine, Switchblade, Pulp Modern,* etc.

She Goes First

by Mary Torson

Lula and Tom have problems. When he's tasked with capturing the moment of death at New York state's execution of Ruth Snyder, it grates on Lula more than she knows. Small wonder she's ready to fly the coop. Torson lives in Milwaukee, Wisconsin with her husband and daughter. She writes mostly historical fiction exploring dark events and the response to them. "To me," she says, "there is nothing more fascinating than a witness."

Tough is a crime fiction website run by Rusty Barnes who publishes stories online for anyone to read. *Tough 2* is the second collection that publishes the work in print. This particular volume is drawn from mid- to late 2018. It's a terrific anthology well worth your support.

Tough 2: Crime Stories
Redneck Press
Editor/Publisher: Rusty Barnes
Contributing Editor: Tim Hennessy
Associate Editor: Rider Barnes
Design: Sue Miller
190 pages, 5" x 8"
POD $14.95
<ToughCrime.com>

Science Fiction Adventures Vol. 1 No. 6 December 1956. Cover by Ed Emshwiller.

Science Fiction Adventures

Royal Publications, New York, NY
Twelve issues
December 1956 to June 1958
First issue: Vol. 1 No. 6 continues numbering from *Suspect Detective Stories*
Second issue: Vol. 1 No. 2 recallibrates numbering from the first issue
5-3/8" x 7-1/2"
128 pages
35¢ cover price

A Classic Error

Article by Steve Carper

"... did you know that you can now buy a full-length book detective novel every month for only 25 cents?"

–Ad copy from the inside front cover of The Mystery Novel of the Month
The Night Before Murder by Steve Fisher 1938

Alex Hillman, born in 1900, graduated from the University of Chicago in 1923 and immediately fell afoul of the wrong crowd: publishers. By 1927 he was situated in that sinkhole of depravity, Greenwich Village. The Hillman Press, under a variety of imprints, published public domain classic erotica. Few suspected that Hillman also was involved with William Godwin Publications, which published current erotica. Titles included *Shameless* and *Unmoral*, the first by Peggy Gaddis and the latter by Jack Woodford, who combined had more than fifty titles printed by several of the sleaze digest publishers of the 1940s. Hillman understood what sold, and to whom. To be fair, a subsidiary named Arcadia House published

"good clean romances." These were aimed at rental libraries, a Depression industry that rented books, mostly genre, at three cents a day to people who could not afford to buy hardcovers. Godwin's sales manager Sam Curl was an expert in this side business. In 1935, they formed another imprint, Hillman-Curl, to cater to this growing market. Hillman-Curl published a bit of everything, from a biography of Kemal Ataturk to *The Complete Fortune Teller*.

Bulbous, balding Alex L. Hillman, to quote a scurrilous *Time* magazine description, was ahead of his time. He saw that publishing paperbacks that were cheap enough for all to afford and could be sold once and for all was a better business than having to chase after

titles that might come back ragged, torn, or wet if they came back at all. Moreover, he realized this before Pocket Books, the first American mass-market-sized paperbacks, hit the market. Hillman's digest lines were patterned closely on Lawrence Spivak's Mercury Press digests but Hillman's distributing experience allowed him to get his paperbacks onto newsstands in the same way that magazines were sold, rather than Spivak's more high-brow reliance on bookstore sales. Hillman Periodicals was founded in 1938 to produce not only these digests but an array of magazines and comic books. Spreading his chips across all the numbers must have seemed a better way to bet that plunging in deep on any type of media, especially when new media types seemed to be springing up every day.

His first line of digests was called The Mystery Novel of the Month. Its first title was Mike Teagle's *Murders in Silk*, a reprint from the hardback published by, let me check my mystery indexes. Hmmm, Hillman-Curl. The next two books, by Steve Fisher and Colver Harris (pseudonym of Anne Colver), were also reprints of Hillman-Curl originals. Other Hillman-Curl authors who Hillman published in the Mystery line include Bernard Newman, Ann Demerest, Sidney Horler, E. R. Punshon, Sutherland Scott, and Paul Haggard. Even mystery fanatics probably don't recognize those names. Spivak snapped up all the stars, leaving Hillman with second- and third-tier performers. Still, if they could sell in hardback, they could sell even better for a mere twenty-five cents in paperback. The imprint stuck around for a full decade, eventually garnering a few major names, among them Craig Rice, Mignon G. Eberhart, and Lawrence Treat.

Those first three volumes were released with no date and no number, but the invaluable Kenneth Johnson dates the latter two

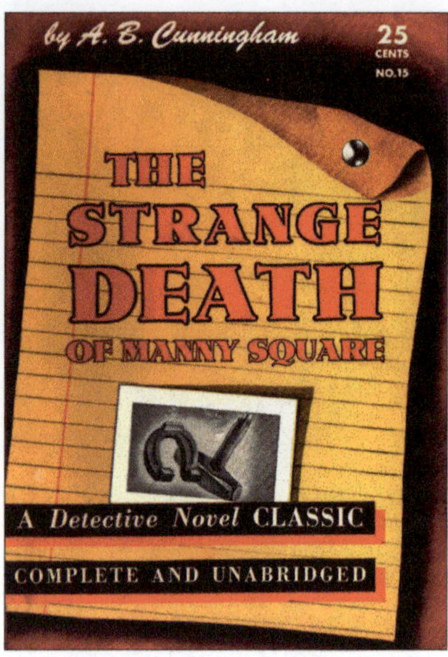

to October and December 1938, making the line technically Mystery Novel of the Bimonthly. (Wikipedia puts the date at 1948. No sources are cited, but the same typo is found in the pulpartists.com biography of Hillman. Don't believe them: that date is simply impossible.) Mystery Novel of the Month finally achieved monthly publication in 1941 and that should have been that, but at the beginning of 1943, starting with No. 41, the line got abruptly renamed The Mystery Novel Classic. At the same time, Hillman rebranded his Western Novel of the Month line to The Western Novel Classic, matching his other three lines, An Adventure Novel Classic, A Thriller Novel Classic, and A Detective Novel Classic. Despite the paper shortages that forced the Mercury Press to drastically slim their fat perfect-bound volumes, Hillman's five lines during the war stayed with the thicker paper that made their releases, despite rigidly hewing to the 128-page, 8-signature length

standard on virtually all digest novels, seem to offer far more reading material for the quarter buck. They slimmed down *after* the war, though, when paper was more available. Perhaps the better, less prone to brown and crumble, paper stock finally became more affordable.

Readers could never doubt that one publisher produced all five lines. They more or less resembled each other, with the series title either in bands across the bottom of the front cover or in boxes at the top. Even more tellingly, their back covers contained no blurbs, only the name of the imprint repeated over and over. The inside back cover normally cross-promoted the lines, reminding a Thriller reader to pick up a Western, or a Western reader to look for a Mystery.

You might think that they would all prominently proclaim they were Hillman Periodicals, but no. Neither Mystery nor Western in the early days ever allowed the name to sully their pages. They originally had no publisher credit at all, but later admitted to being Novel Selections, and postwar releases did plaster "Hillman Publications" on the cover. Thriller was Novel Selections, Inc. from the start. Adventure and Detective scorned such deceptions. They had Hillman in all-caps on the title page. (Other descriptors did slip in. I've seen Mystery Book of the Month, e.g. I only have about half of the 345 books in these lines and other surprises may lurk there. However, these generalities work well to distinguish the lines. Why Hillman worked so hard to connect the lines while obscuring their common origin constitutes another western-world thrilling detective mystery adventure.)

Hillman junked all his crime magazines and comic books in 1944 to reserve enough paper to launch *Pageant* magazine, a photo-heavy digest that was supposed to compete with the king of all magazines, *Reader's Digest*, but instead fought it out with the second-tier *Coronet*. None of the three carried advertising, so circulation meant everything. *Pageant* debuted with 500,000 copies, probably sold half that many, and thereby lost huge amounts of money. It lasted until 1977, so Hillman eventually made it profitable but it must have been a huge distraction for its first struggling years.

The fiction digests had settled into steady sellers with a standardized promotional format. Each inside back cover was slugged with the same paragraph.

NOVEL CLASSICS offers you five reading treats each month – a choice of the best in each of the following five fields: Mystery, Adventure, Thriller, Detective and Western. Watch for the newest selections!

The rest of the page blurbed a title from another of the lines. Here's an example. Sometime in 1945, judging from the few clues Johnson has pieced together, Hillman released *Journey to Murder*, Adventure Novel Classic No. 34, by Robert Portner Koehler, a reprint of 1944's *Salute to Murder*, published in hardcover by the Phoenix Press. It told readers to *"Be Sure to Read the Latest Mystery Novel Classic,"* which was *Terror by Twilight*, Mystery Novel Classic No. 70, by Kathleen Moore Knight, originally published in 1942 by Doubleday, Doran, several steps up the ladder of publishing renown

from Phoenix. *Terror's* inside back cover blurbed Thriller Novel Classic No. 31, Vera Kelsey's *Fear Came First*, and so on around the chain.

Whether all five titles appeared simultaneously or dribbled out through the month is unknown. Hillman jobbed out all his printing rather than owning presses, so he had to rely on outsiders to function. The logistics of printing five books each month must have been daunting. If each digest title had press runs of 100,000, a guess that's probably conservative considering that mass-market paperbacks regularly printed twice that many, half a million covers had to be churned out every month in addition to *Pageant's* half million. Printers would hardly get to take a break before stripping the plates from one set of covers, cleaning out the lines, refreshing the ink, and starting the next set. Almost any inattentiveness, distraction, laziness, or communications snafu could

ROBERT PORTNER KOEHLER
Mystery NOVEL
25 CENTS NO. 34
CLASSIC
MURDER
terror by twilight
An Adventure Novel CLASSIC
A FULL LENGTH NOVEL
by Kathleen Moore Knight
A HILLMAN PUBLICATION

THE Mystery NOVEL
25 CENTS NO. 70
CLASSIC
terror by twilight
A FULL LENGTH DETECTIVE NOVEL
by Kathleen Moore Knight

ruin a run and send thousands of spoiled covers to the junkyard. Printers had to be very good and experienced while quality checkers needed to be quick and observant.

In hindsight, 1945 must have been a low point for both trades. Somewhere around 16,000,000 Americans served in the Armed Forces, decimating all non-essential industries. Back-ups, former retirees, and tyros abounded, with all of them nevertheless pushed to top speed. If there were any time, a historian would point to as likely to see a sharp uptick in printing errors, early 1945 would be the consensus choice.

And here's the evidence. Somehow the cover for Koehler's *Journey to Murder* got printed on top of the cover of Knight's *Terror by Twilight*. Staring at it makes your eyes hurt, and gives you sympathy for the haunted pair of eyes looking out from the chaos. The double printing goes all the way around to the spine and the back cover, a mish-mosh of black text that resembles early abstract impressionism. The interior pages are all Koehler; only the cover suffered.

No history attaches to the volume, no explanation can be found for how and why this odd printing mistake ever escaped into the wild. Was this pulled from the press run and handed to a furious Hillman so he could blister the plant manager for his carelessness? Did it make its way out of the printing plant and land on an unsuspecting newsstand? Was it returned as unusable and rescued by an employee who kept it as a souvenir? Or did some hurried commuter grab it on the way to a late train home, not caring

that the cover was one-of-a-kind?

The latter is a possibility. When I received the double-printing from the seller, I pulled the two original digests from my shelves to do a close comparison. To my surprise, I realized for the first time that the Knight I already owned was *itself* a misprint, a bad registration error that made the cover type resemble a 3-D print before one puts the red-blue glasses on. I never noticed, merely checking the number off in my spreadsheet. If two different errors can be associated with the same title, the scene inside the printing plant must have resembled a slapstick comedy run at high speed. If ever there were a good reason to yell "Stop the presses" the day that *Terror by Twilight* self-destructed is it.

Alex Hillman somehow pulled himself together after this fiasco and continued publishing digests, although he evidently noticed a subtle shift in the market. In 1947 he killed three of the five lines, leaving only the Mystery and Western Novel Classic imprints alive. He augmented them by starting two new lines that year, Fighting Western Novel and Western Action Novel, which was renamed Gunfire Action Novel with No. 5. The Mystery Novel Classic line sputtered out probably in 1948. All three western lines wound up on Boot Hill in 1951. Spotting another market trend, Hillman launched *Worlds Beyond* in 1950, a digest-sized science fiction magazine edited by Damon Knight. According to legend, the magazine was killed as soon as the sales figures for the first issue reached the front office.

Hillman saw the light. He found the true booming market, that of men's magazines. His titles included

THE
Mystery NOVEL
CLASSIC

25 CENTS
NO. 70

terror
by
twilight

A FULL LENGTH
DETECTIVE NOVEL

by Kathleen Moore Knight

TERROR BY TWILIGHT · MYSTERY NOVEL CLASSIC · 70

ROBERT PORTNER KOEHLER

25 CENTS
NO. 34

JOURNEY TO
MURDER

An *Adventure* Novel CLASSIC

A FULL LENGTH NOVEL

A HILLMAN PUBLICATION

JOURNEY TO MURDER · An Adventure Novel CLASSIC · 34

Action For Men, Epic, Exposé For Men, Champ, Escape To Adventure, and *Real Adventure Magazine.* All of them featured brawny men and half-dressed women on their covers, suffering imaginative torments: pulp magazines in all but name. The only difference was that the fictions published by fast-typing authors purported to be non-fiction accounts. None of these titles, to my knowledge, were digests.

Hillman retired in 1961, selling *Pageant* to Macfadden Publications. Until his early death in 1968 he concentrated on his notable collection of modern art, including, ironically, many abstract impressionists. I wonder if an overprint of Koehler/ Knight resides in a museum, acclaimed as a forgotten masterpiece.

Worlds Beyond Vol. 1 No. 2 January 1951

Steve Carper's comprehensive history, *Robots In American Popular Culture,* has been released. A companion site <RobotsInAmericanPopularCulture.com> contains more than 350 robot-related images and links to over 50 additional articles on robots. The url site for all his future history is <FlyingCarsandFoodPills.com>. Steve's digest novel collection has passed 1250.

Skyworlds-Science Fiction Classics No. 1 November 1977

Skyworlds
Science Fiction Classics *(first two)*
Skyworlds Marvels in Science Fiction (last two)
Humorama Inc., Rockville Centre, NY
Four issues
November 1977 to August 1978
5-3/8" x 7-1/4"
82 pages
75¢ cover price

When the Butterfly Emerged From the Cocoon

Article by Ward Smith

"Any collector who has a complete run knows how much a thousand issues are. My run fills nearly eleven meters of shelving. I can't store them all in one place because, during its eighty-five years, *Astounding/Analog* (hereinafter simplified to *ASF*) has kept changing size, from pulp to letter-size, back to pulp, then digest, then semi-slick, and then various gradations of digest."

"The Analog Millennium" by Mike Ashley *Analog Science Fiction and Fact* June 2015

The "digest-size" selected for many publications interests me. I grew up with magazines of varying sizes, from the super-large weeklies *Life* and *Look* and the so-called "pulps" to the very efficient, easy-to-handle/store/shelve modern digest size. Perhaps one of the best representations of changes leading to digest-size is that of *Astounding Stories/Science Fiction/Analog Science Fact and Fiction*, and so on.

***Astounding* formats (shown in relative scale)**
Cover images from Galactic Central.

Astounding Stories March 1933

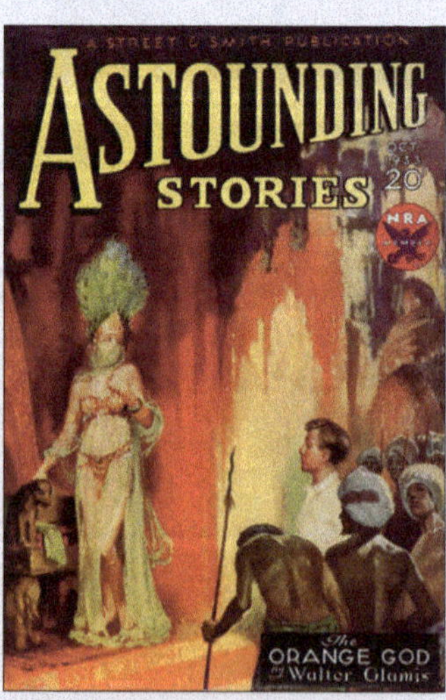

Astounding Stories October 1933

That venerable periodical began life nearly 90 years ago in January 1930 as *Astounding Stories of Super Science*, published by Clayton Publications. It was a 7" x 10" "pulp," with untrimmed edges. A monthly, it lasted through the March 1933 issue until money problems caught up with it.

Someone, however, saw promise in this magazine. Street & Smith (S&S) Publishers bought it during the summer of 1933 and brought out *Astounding Stories* in October of that year as a 7" x 10" pulp.

The cocoon began to split when *Astounding* changed the format to 6.5" x 9.5" with trimmed page edges in May 1936. S&S then hired the now-legendary (and late) John W. Campbell, Jr. as editor in October 1937, effective with the December 1937 issue. One of Campbell's first acts was to update the magazine's title to *Astounding Science Fiction*.

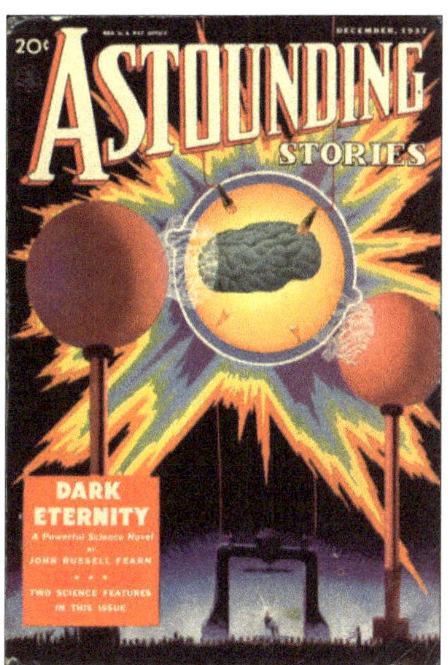

Astounding Stories December 1937

Bedsheet

From January 1942 to April 1943 *Astounding* changed to 8.5" x 11" ("bedsheet") size, with 128

Astounding Stories May 1936

Astounding Science Fiction January 1942

Astounding Science Fiction January 1942

WW II began to have an impact on publications. The July 1942 issue was the first of only a few non-science fiction front covers the magazine ever ran, this one being the American flag in a Charles de Feo photo (mistakenly credited to Hubert Rogers at the time but corrected in the September issue).

While he was still able to get good material from the likes of Isaac Asimov, A.E. van Vogt, and Fredric Brown, Campbell began his "Probability Zero" short-short story series to try to enlist new writers with innovative ideas (April 1942). In August the mag ran the last front cover by Rogers until 1947, as he had enlisted in the Canadian Armed Forces. Robert A. Heinlein was conspicuously absent as he was involved serving the U.S. Navy. The front cover artist of choice from December 1942 to January 1947 was William Timmins.

trimmed pages, and a price of 25 cents (after 11 years at 20 cents per copy). Bedsheet has the same dimensions as a standard sheet of typewriter paper (in the U.S.A.).

Astounding formats (shown in relative scale)
Cover images from Galactic Central.

Astounding Science Fiction May 1943

Astounding Science Fiction November 1943

Astounding Science Fiction July 1942

Unknown March 1939

In May 1943 *ASF* returned to 7" x 10" pulp size, 162 pages. It stayed like that through the October issue.

It was sometime during this period, that science fiction got a boost from the United States government itself. Federal agents visited John W. Campbell's editorial offices, so the story goes, to ask questions about a story in a recent *ASF* issue by Cleve Cartmill. Apparently, Mr. Cartmill had described fairly accurately a top-secret nuclear triggering device then being developed at Los Alamos as part of the Manhattan Project. As it turned out (later), the device's description was simply a matter of logic and luck on the author's part, but the incident was used to exemplify to neophytes the sometimes prophetic nature of science fiction.

A Venture into the *Unknown* 1939–1943

The story isn't complete without mentioning John W. Campbell's dipping into the realm of fantasy. *Un-*known was the place for a category of fiction that was well written, had at least a reasonably plausible plot, was entertaining—"*and did not fit into the thematic boundaries of speculative (science) fiction that otherwise qualified for* Astounding."

The magazine was still greatly lamented (with hopes for its revival at any moment) within segments of fandom as late as 1954, eleven years after its demise. The only fan following that may rival this is for *Weird Tales*. *Unknown* remains among the most respected magazines of its type ever published.

Street & Smith/Campbell had launched *Unknown* as a trimmed pulp (just like *Astounding*) in March 1939. The title additive "Fantasy Fiction" appeared with the February 1940 issue, and it was retitled to *Unknown Worlds Fantasy Fiction* in October 1941. It was published monthly through December 1940, then bimonthly. In October 1941 it went to 8.5" x 11.5" bedsheet-size and stayed that way until April 1943, when it returned to pulp size for its last three issues. After 39 issues, it died with the October 1943 number.

As it was on its way out—probably sacrificed to the World War II paper shortages that threatened both it and *Astounding*—what proved to be its last issue proclaimed that the next issue (December 1943, which was never published) would be in a new, convenient "pocket book" size.

What that really meant was "digest" size, and—indeed—*Astounding* made that radical change at the same time, but *Unknown* perished in the transition. *Unknown* was revived as a bedsheet one-shot anthology called From *Unknown Worlds—An Anthology of Modern Fantasy for Grownups* in 1948.

Format Change—
Yes, Size Matters

Astounding shook up the pulp magazine world when it changed format radically with the November 1943 issue: it went to "pocket book" size (as Campbell described it) or more accurately, "digest" size—dubbed so after *Reader's Digest*, which was founded in 1922.

Campbell also added a "roto-gravure" insert (slick-paper pages suitable for printing photo features). These pages utilized typeface and halftone pics in sepia tone until the end of 1945, then after that, in standard black-and-white. The rotogravure pages were used for printing markedly improved illustrations to accompany science articles by astronomer Dr. R.S. Richardson, scientist Willy Ley, engineer George O. Smith, and (PhD physicist) Campbell himself writing under the Arthur McCann pen name.

While the smaller-sized, now-178-page magazine did not immediately alter the pulp-sf ambiance after the first shock, it did sound the death knell for the old ragged-edged popular pulp magazines. The new *Astounding* was 75% the size of its pulp predecessor, but contained approximately 9% more pages.

The final emergence of the butterfly into digest-sized glory occurred with the introduction of *Avon Fantasy Reader* in 1947, *The Magazine of Fantasy* (later adding *Science Fiction*) in Fall 1949, and *Galaxy Science Fiction* in October 1950. The butterfly had spread its wings and taken flight.

Ward Smith is a pen name used by a collector of vintage books with paper wraps, including Armed Services Editions, original Pocket Books, Dell "Mapbacks," and some early wartime digests.

the best of bare•bones

Edited by
Peter Enfantino and
John Soleri

6" x 9" 240 pages
Cimarron Street Books,
Oct. 2019
Trade Paperback

Companion Website:
<barebonesez.blogspot.com>

Robots in American Popular Culture

by Steve Carper

7" x 10" 300 pages
McFarland Books,
June 2019
Trade Paperback
and Kindle

Companion Website
<robotsinamerican
popularculture.com>

Buckthorn Justice

Fantasy Fiction by John Kuharik
Illustration by Rick McCollum

"He'd gotten his nickname for looting boots off a debtor who had committed suicide days before they'd come to serve a warrant."

Lars stood before the bench in the dim courtroom while the judge signed warrants.

The red epaulets on his immaculate black leather armor identified him as Captain of the Watch. His ramrod posture, and crisp manner of speaking identified him as ex-military.

The man next to him was Felles, a cousin of the Buckthorn Borough Mayor, and the newly appointed Debt Sheriff. His diamond rings and constant smirk suggested he was a man with political protection. His attire, a mix of Saturday night tavern chic, and ornate shortsword, suggested a para-military poser.

Lars was responsible for executing the warrants on real criminals. Felles handled the ones for debtors, who once arrested, would be indentured without trial to a workhouse—usually for the rest of their lives.

Many of the debtors were veterans of the Gnoll War who needed money to rebuild their lives or heal their wounds, but had borrowed from predators who charged high interest and were quick to foreclose, often after a single missed payment.

The judge gave over the signed warrants.

Felles scurried out to where his posse waited for assignments.

He called to his first deputy—a wiry sort named NoEar, for having lost his right one in a street brawl. "Here," he said, "Brother and sister farmers this side of the river. In their twenties. Take Deadboots with you. Should be easy for you two."

Deadboots sidled up to No-Ear to get a look at the warrants. His pinched face a display of eager anticipation. He'd gotten his nickname for looting boots off a debtor who had committed suicide days before they'd come to serve a warrant. NoEar pushed him away with his elbow, "Get off me you smelly sod, you can't even read."

Lars watched them laugh and spar with each other as they saddled horses. Undisciplined swine. He turned to Felles as they rode away, "You trust those guys?"

"They work cheap."

Lars, shook his head, and was about to head for his office, but stopped, "By the way, Felles, have you seen my dog?"

"What?"

"I asked if you've seen my dog. Don't pretend you don't know my dog. Black and brown shepherd?"

Felles shook his head, and looked sideways at his men. "Why ask me?"

Snickers from the posse.

"Cause he went missing about the time your boys started hanging around here."

"Maybe he's holed up with a bitch."

The posse exploded with laughter. "Maybe you should offer a reward, Captain."

Lars glared. "I'll remind you, in this Borough, dog theft is the same as horse theft."

NoEar and Deadboots reached the farm midafternoon. A house sat off to the left, a barn to the right. Dismounting without seeing anyone, they pulled cudgels from their saddles. NoEar signaled he would take the house and indicated Deadboots take the barn. He always tried to be the one to find to the woman first.

The barn door was open when 'Boots reached it. He heard activity inside. When his eyes adjusted to the shade, he saw a man unloading hops from a wagon onto drying racks.

"I'm looking for Blair," he announced.

"I'm him," said a sandy-haired man in overalls and brown shirt.

"I have a warrant for your arrest."

The guy turned with a noticeable limp. Easier, and easier, thought 'Boots.

"Run, Millie, Run!" Blair screamed as loud as he could. 'Boots nailed him on the side of his head with his club. That cut off the scream, and dropped Blair to the barn floor.

Millie was shucking corn in the chicken coop behind the house. Same colored hair, only longer, she wore cotton work pants and yellow shirt. Hearing Blair's scream she immediately thought gnoll attack. The paring knife in her pocket wouldn't do much good, but the four pronged spade leaning against the house would. She snatched it up as she raced toward for the barn.

NoEar appeared from around the side of the house as she passed. He knocked the spade from her hand with his club and grabbed her hair. "You're under arrest," he said, twisting her head up close. Stale sausage breath and spittle hit her face. "But, let's go into the house for some fun first."

He was still grinning at her as she brought the paring knife from her pocket to stick its point under his chin. "Let me go, or I'll kill you." It was a hopeful bluff, since she had never even killed a chicken for dinner.

NoEar froze for a second, but sensed her lack of commitment. He clamped his hand around hers and bent her wrist back. The knife fell, and he laughed, but stopped short when she headbutted him in the nose.

"Bitch," he yelled, stepping back. But before she could do anything else, 'Boots came from behind and thumped her on the head with his club. She fell into the dust.

"You know they don't want us messing with the women."

"Shut up, and remember who you're talking to." Embarrassed both by being wounded by a woman and chided by an inferior, NoEar kicked Millie in the stomach as she lay there. He wiped his bloody nose on his sleeve and felt it with his fingers. "Did you get the guy?"

"I did. And they have a wagon. Wanna use it?"

Still trying to straighten his nose, he said, "yeah, tie 'em up, as usual. I'll be back in a minute." He went into the house found the wash bowl and got most of the blood off his face. He took a towel to hold to his nose, and looked until he found a bottle of whisky.

Deadboots stepped close to Millie's face, and the odor had the effect of smelling salts. Her eyes popped open. Her head felt like it had exploded. She stilled herself and suppressed a groan, thinking it might be a good idea to play dead and bide time.

Her hip bone was pressing against something underneath her. She slowly realized it was the paring knife. The boots had stepped out of sight, so she took a chance no one was watching, and slowly reached under herself, and slipped the knife into a pocket. She passed out again and came to when someone pulled at her arms and tied her hands behind her. Also her ankles. With grunting and cursing, the men rolled her over, being sure to feel her up pretty good in the process, before taking her by armpits and ankles and slinging her up onto the load of hops next to her brother.

She endured it without reacting.

She fell against Blair's back. She whispered to him, but he didn't answer or move.

The collectors tied their own horses to the back of the wagon and climbed up front where they began to pass the whisky back and forth. Millie squirmed around on the scratchy bed of dried hops trying to find out if Blair was breathing. Finally, she got her ear against his back, and was thankful to hear his heart beating.

Darkness closed in as they approached the the edge of the Borough, and by that time Millie had decided if she rode into the workhouse with Blair, they would both be in a fix forever. If she escaped, she could get help and free him later. She fretted over the idea of escaping without him. It seemed disloyal, but she finally decided it really wasn't.

The two up front were singing loudly. She inched her way over to the edge of the wagon, crunching the hops, grateful the wind overhead in the trees covered the sound. The sides of the wagon were about eighteen inches high, and the load of hops reached a level just under that. Even with her ankles tied, she got a knee above the edge first, then levered her whole leg over. The other leg went over more easily, and suddenly she knew she had passed the point of no return. More of her weight was outside the wagon than in. As she dangled there, edge pressing into her stomach, hands tied behind her back, she contemplated her next move. She needed to fling herself backward with enough force to clear the edge, and not hit her chin or fall under the wheels.

She took a breath and turned

her head, and heaved herself up and back as hard she could. She landed on her back head-first down the embankment. She lay stunned for a few minutes, until the blood pounding in her head forced her to squirm upright.

Flexible and fit, she sat through her arms and pulled her tied wrists down the backs of her legs and over her feet. Once she had them in front of her, it was a simple matter of using the paring knife to cut her restraints. She felt new pains everywhere, but she could stand and move. She scrambled into the tangle of scrub oaks and low pines that lined the road. She knew where to go, but it would be slow getting there. Her wrecked body refused to run.

When the wagon arrived at the workhouse without the woman, Felles went into a rage and wailed on NoEar, and Deadboots with his baton. "Get out of my sight, you useless drunks." He pointed to two other men. "Baldo, Fred, you're up." He handed them the warrant. "Its almost dark, use the dog."

Baldo, a hulk of a man, got his name from having no hair anywhere on his body, not even eyelids and lashes. Fred, new to the posse, and average looking had no nickname yet.

"What's she look like?" Baldo asked NoEar as he crawled away wincing from the baton blows.

His answer was a slurred nasal tone.

Baldo bent lower to hear better. "What?"

Baldo listened again and interpreted for Fred, "He says, a blond bitch in a yellow shirt."

They strapped on swords and lit a torch. Fred clipped the shepherd's collar to a long lead and made him jump onto the wagon to get Millie's scent. They mounted up and followed as the dog sniffed from one side of the road to the other, until it stopped where Millie had left the wagon. When her trail entered brush too thick for the horses, the men dismounted, tied them to saplings, and followed the dog on foot.

Millie scrambled out of the brush into Uncle Grigg's neighborhood near total exhaustion.

Totally dark now, the place looked nothing like what it had when she played there as a kid before the war. Mortar fire had turned several blocks of cottages into a skeletal skyline of broken chimneys, and blanketed the ground with shattered glass and masonry that crunched underfoot. She headed straight for Uncle Grigg's house, one of a few with only minor damage. Seeing no light in the window, she worried he wouldn't be home.

The barking dog behind her seemed louder.

The squeak of his back door hinge caused Grigg to grab his sword and sit up in bed. Motionless, he listened until he heard a floorboard creak, then he stood. Cursing himself for not having double-checked the lock, he stepped out of his bedroom and flattened himself against the wall next to his wardrobe.

The dying embers in the fireplace cast only the dimmest of light, but enough for him to see a slight figure near the kitchen table, leaning with a hand on the back of a chair. He heard heavy breathing and caught the glint of a knife in one hand.

He was fast for a guy with a six foot frame. In three steps he grabbed the wrist holding the knife and was about to crack a head with the butt of his sword when the person looked up. The perfect face and sandy blond hair brought instant recognition.

"Millie?" he said, barely stopping himself.

She flinched as she gasped for breath.

"What are you doing sneaking in? I almost killed you."

She pointed to the door. Grigg froze.

Outside, Fred choked up on the leash and yanked it to rile the dog. Baldo took the torch from him, and asked, "Know who lives here?"

"No idea."

"Well, they're harboring an escapee. We take 'em all, dead or alive."

He burst through the door. A sword in one hand and torch in the other. He saw Grigg was armed and took a vicious swing that would have taken a slower man's head off. Grigg responded with a battlecry, and a carefully aimed stab at the man's belly, which was deflected by a downward swing of the torch. Millie picked up her paring knife and rolled under the table. Grigg feinted with his sword, and aimed a kick at a knee. The man jumped sideways, the kick landed in the air causing Grigg to hop stupidly on his other foot to retain balance. He cursed himself as his opponent grinned and stepped inside of Grigg's swing. But, Grigg elbowed him square in the teeth with a satisfying crunch. The man staggered, but before Grigg could follow up, Fred stepped through the door unhooked the leash and yelled, "Kill."

The dog didn't move, even after Fred yelled kill again and flailed him with the leash.

Grigg backed toward a corner to keep his opponents in front of him.

Next door, in the workshop where Grigg repaired and sold weapons, his hired man, Doth, was sleeping on a cot. He had his own place across town, but slept here whenever the men planned an early scavenging trip—like the one today. He woke to Grigg's battle cry and knew it meant a fight to the death.

Grabbing the first sword his hand came to on the dark workbench, he stepped into a pair of old shoes and bolted outside. Damn, he'd picked up a broken broadsword, thick but with only fourteen inches of blade. Running towards Grigg's door he heard swords clanging and reached it seconds after Fred and the dog went in. He didn't know how many attackers there were, but he knew this was one. He got to Fred as he yelled kill the second time, and had raised his arm to strike the dog again. Doth chopped off the leash hand at the wrist and grabbed the dog's collar.

Fred screamed and held up his new stump which spurted blood in his face. Doth didn't wait for nature to take its course. He backhanded Fred's forehead with the flat side of his blade. That dropped him like a sack of rats, body jerking while it bled out.

Seeing Grigg had the other man well in hand, he couched and stroked the dog while whispering calming sounds in one ear.

Grigg punched Baldo in the face with his free hand and pushed him away. From under the table, Millie stabbed her knife through the toe of his shoe, pinning his foot to the floor. He cursed, and tried to step back, but lost balance and fell, striking his head on the edge of the hearth. Blood ran from an ear. Grigg stepped up to run him through the chest, but the man was dead already.

Grigg scanned the room, and said to Doth, "You had to chop off a hand? Look at all that blood on my floor."

"Sorry boss, it seemed the thing to do." He grinned while he continued to pet the now calm animal.

Grigg snorted. "Well, when you finish playing with your new dog, how about dragging these clowns out and cleaning the floor."

"Sure thing." The dog let Doth guide it back to the workshop, where he tied it to the workbench and gave it water and a crusty biscuit. He didn't notice the dog ignore both.

Millie raised herself into a chair "What's this about?" Grigg asked, pulling her knife from the intruder's shoe.

"Its Blair," she sobbed, "They took him."

"Who took him?"

"Debt collectors. They had warrants."

"These guys?" Grigg pointed at the bodies on the floor.

"Not them, but ones like them."

Millie's mother, also named Millie, was Grigg's sister. She had married his friend Conly who had inherited his father's farm. The couple soon had Blair and Millie, and a hard-working but reasonable life until the Gnoll attacks. Conly joined Grigg and thousands of Buckthorn Borough citizen-soldiers who left everything behind to fight the gnolls. Conly never returned from the final battle across the river.

Grigg had helped the fatherless family rebuild the farm, leaving only after they seemed on their feet. Later, the older Millie took sick with a cough. Her funeral, two years ago, marked the last time Grigg had seen the kids.

Grigg put his sword on the table. Millie placed his hidden key beside it. He nodded, understanding how she had gotten in.

He lit a candle from the fireplace embers, got her a cup of water, then pulled up a chair for himself.

"If these two were able to follow you here, others will too."

"We have to get my brother."

"We will. How much do you owe?"

"Lots," she sobbed.

He pointed to blood on her shirt. "Are you hurt?"

"Hurt? I've been hit, kicked, tied, fondled, and flung backwards off a wagon. The blood is from the guy I headbutted. Then there's this." She guided his hand to a lump on her head. Next she showed the bruise on her ribs where NoEar had kicked her.

Grigg directed her to the facilities where she could wash, and went to find her a clean shirt. When she returned, he asked again about the money.

"Three thousand gold."

Grigg choked. "What the hell Millie? That's a fortune. Last I counted, I maybe have two hundred." He paused. "And if I sold every sword and war relic I have, I might come up with another hundred, tops."

She buried her face in her hands and cried furiously. "Mom borrowed hundreds for a healer for her cough. It went on so long. The first year of the drought we had a bad crop and got behind in payments." She shrugged. "And now here we are."

Grigg knew how it went after that. "I'm really sorry I don't have the money."

She wiped tears with the sleeve of her borrowed shirt, sandy curls framing her face. She smiled faintly. "I didn't expect you would. But, Mom said if ever we got in trouble, 'go see Uncle Grigg.'"

"I miss your Mom."

He sighed, then jerked a thumb at Doth, who had returned to collect the bodies. "Meet Doth. He's been working with me a couple years."

The young people smiled and touched forearms in greeting, Doth apologizing for his bloody hands. Millie guessed he was about her age, and thanked him for helping save her.

"The debt posse will soon be here looking for these guys," said Grigg, "We'll go to Doth's place as soon as we clean up." He suggested she lay down for a bit and she did.

Grigg packed gear and saddled the horses. Doth dragged the dead men out and dumped them down a ruined well a block away. He threw a bucket of water on Grigg's floor-boards, and finished by sweeping pine boughs across the blood trails.

Doth's place was in the one corner room left of a destroyed inn. Once there, the trio tried to get a few hours of sleep. Millie took the only bed, moaning occasion-ally from her wounds. The men took the floor on blankets—Grigg wide-eyed in the dark, working out plans—Doth snoring content-edly. The dog lay near Millie's bed, chin on paws, eyes open.

Millie and Doth woke to find Grigg had already been to the workhouse and back. "Blair's been sent to a lumber camp south of Hadley's Corner," he reported. "And I was followed here, but I lost them."

Millie looked worried. "My head hurts and I don't feel like myself."

"If we hurry, we should be able to get you across the river, get Blair from the camp, and then have Doth guide you to the settlements on the frontier. You know you can't stay in Buckthorn anymore."

"I know. The farm's ruined for us anyway," she said be-fore falling back to sleep.

"She doesn't seem like she could run the tunnel this morning," said Doth.

"I've seen her kind of head injury before," said Grigg. "She's not climbing up and down river-banks for a boat crossing either."

They decided she should dress up to impersonate a noble, and cross the bridge in a carriage. And when she woke later, feeling a little better, she said she could do that.

Doth pulled out a trunk of disguises.

"You've done this before," she said from behind a screen as she changed clothes.

Doth caught a glimpse of bare shoulder, and decided she was cuter than he first thought.

"We earn more smug-gling people across the river than we do scavenging."

Soon, Millie was dressed as *Squire Madson*, a lord from the upper castle. Resplendent in white leather, he sported a pow-der blue ascot and matching hat pierced with a long bird plum.

Doth, in high boots, and coach-man's cap, presented as a common footman. As a final touch, the dog wore a shiny chain collar.

Doth helped Millie into the carriage, the dog followed and promptly curled up at her feet. "Remember, Doth said, "If it goes bad, I'll open either door and we jump off the bridge that side. I'll have a cushion that floats."

Sweat ran down her back, and she decided not to mention she couldn't swim.

At the bridge, a line of freight wagons waited at the checkpoint to pay tolls. Guards with pikes and crossbows stood at usual positions.

Doth knew noblemen never waited in the line. He pulled around and forward, then called loudly, "Squire Madson traveling to his vineyard." In truth, they were heading for a vineyard, albeit an abandoned one, near Hadley's Corner.

He handed over the expected gratuity.

The guard replied, "That's very kind of your master, but I have to look inside today, no matter who it is."

When he opened the door he saw Millie, dressed like a man, legs crossed like a man, looking down her nose at him, like any other nobleman he'd ever encountered. She looked pale, but didn't they all? He gave a two finger salute, eyes lingering only on the dog. Millie's pits were pouring sweat by the time the man closed the door.

"Proceed."

Grigg, meantime had ridden ahead to Hadley's Corner, left his horse at the livery, then went to the tavern. The owner, Merk, was a war buddy of his. They hoisted a few beers and caught up on each other's lives, until at a natural lull in the conversation, Grigg asked, "Workhouse wagons come through here earlier?"

"Yeah. Guards came in to eat, left them poor buggers out in the sun."

"How far's that new lumber camp?"

"Close enough the guards come here evenings to drink." Merk looked curiously at his friend. "Why did you really come here?"

"Want to help me spring a veteran's kid?"

"Absolutely," said Merk, drying glasses from the lunch crowd. "And I know just how."

"Do tell."

"They don't have a full contingent of guards yet. The sergeant is a big lush, brings them all here except for one at the main entrance and one at the workers tent."

Grigg caught on. "You'll keep them here with free drinks, I'll do the rest."

Merk smiled, "You got it, except for the free drinks part. I'll dope the pricks if they try to leave early."

That evening Grigg waited until he saw the guards arrive at the tavern, then walked to the camp. Merk had been right. He avoided the main entrance, circled around, and caught the guard dozing at the workers tent. He clunked him to make sure, and lifted his key. Inside, moving among a jumble of sleeping bodies, he whispered for Blair, until the man answered.

"Uncle Grigg?"

"Who else?" he said grinning. He unlocked Blair's shackle, and handed the key to another prisoner who had woken. "Help the others," he said.

"Millie?" asked Blair.

"Safe. Banged up a bit, but safe. You'll see her soon."

They followed Grigg out the way he'd come. At the livery they double mounted Grigg's horse and rode to the vineyard.

Watching from the shadows, Felles said, "I knew it." He called to NoEar, DeadBoots, and two others, "Let's go."

Grigg led his horse down the wooded lane into an building holding large wine vats. He tied his horse near Doth's carriage. At the back wall they climbed narrow stairs to a loft. A dim candle on a wooden crate, the only light. As soon as she saw him, Millie, who had changed into her own clothes, threw herself at Blair. They hugged and laughed joyously even as Grigg shushed them.

The value of the loft as a hiding spot was that it afforded a view of any one approaching, and the narrow staircase was defendable by one man. This only worked if someone was watching. Felles and company got to the top of the stairs while the group was celebrating.

The attackers drew swords and fanned out as Felles said, "We have an arrest warrant for the girl, and we are taking the escapee as well. I don't know who you are, but stand back and you won't get hurt."

"No one's going anywhere with you," said Grigg, nodding to Doth.

Doth bent down and said something none could hear, and suddenly the dog sprang from hiding onto the chest of the man nearest the top of the stairs. Man and dog tumbled down the stairs screaming and snarling.

Grigg slammed his sword blade down on the candle, pitching the loft into complete darkness. Grigg pushed Blair and Millie behind a pile of crates. "Stay down."

Grigg crept left along a row of crates he and Doth had arranged for such an event. Doth went right and they came out behind the attackers. But the surprise was spoiled when Boots lit a torch and exposed them. Now, Felles and three men faced Doth and Grigg. Millie and Blair were concealed behind the attackers.

NoEar and Boots pressed the center attack. Felles and the torch holder behind them took opportune stabs at their flanks. Outnumbered, Grigg and Doth began to falter, when, suddenly, the commotion at the bottom of the stairs quieted, and the dog re-appeared at the top, bloody, and growling. It leaped, clamping jaws onto the torchman's sword arm. The man backed against the crates, where Blair reached out from hiding to put a chokehold on him. He flailed with the torch and Blair felt the heat singe his face, but held his grip until the guy passed out. NoEar fell back to protect his downed friend and took a swing at Blair.

Millie saw that and went berserk. "I've had enough of you," she said, reaching from the crates to slash his cheek with her paring knife. That distracted him enough for Doth to slice his throat.

Felles decided he didn't like the odds any more, and poser that he was, jumped from the loft. Boots, noticing he'd been abandoned, said "Screw this," and followed his boss over the edge.

"We won?" asked Blair, of his equally incredulous companions.

"Yeah, but Felles has more men than those. Kill the light, and let's go," said Grigg.

They clambered down the stairs stepping over the mangled man at the bottom. Blair and Millie got into the carriage with the dog, Doth took the reins up front. Grigg led the way to the main road. When they emerged from the wooded lane, they found themselves encircled by a dozen or more torch-bearing figures on horseback. Felles lay dead face up on the road.

NoEar and several of the debt posse sat in a row, hands tied behind them.

Grigg heard a familiar voice order him to dismount. He hesitated, then did so. Lars approached from the darkness behind the horses, red epaulets clearly in view. The men were not friends. Grigg disapproved of his leadership style. Lars thought him lacking in respect for authority. But, they were both veterans from the same war and shared a camaraderie that sticks for life.

"What do you want, Lars?" Grigg said quietly.

The Captain looked him over. "As insolent as ever, but it seems you rescued my dog."

"*Your* dog?"

"My dog. The shepherd. The one in that carriage with the *lord*."

"Damn," said Grigg, "How many spies do you have?"

"No spies, just honest, observant citizens."

Grigg called to the carriage. "Let the dog out."

The dog bounded over to Lars, who hunched down for hugs and licks, unfazed by its bloody jaws.

Grigg waited a respectful moment. "What's his name?"

"No name. Doesn't need me to give him a name to know who he is."

"He's ferocious."

"He's unusual—never seen him eat," said Lars as he remounted his horse, and wheeled around.

"I suspected the posse had the dog, but no proof until someone saw them bring it out to chase the woman. We tracked them to your house, but you were gone. I wondered how you were involved, until I figured it was your niece and nephew the posse was after. Next day when they followed you after you visited the workhouse, we followed them, and here we are."

"And where exactly is here?" asked Grigg.

"You be my witness at the dog thieves trial," he said, spinning away on his horse, "The carriage is free to go."

After The Watch left, Grigg shook hands with Doth. "See you in six months?"

Doth glanced at Millie, "Maybe more."

Millie and Blair group-hugged their uncle, and Millie whispered, "Mom would have said that was a spirit dog come to help us."

"I remember. And I used to argue with her when she talked like that."

"You wouldn't argue today, would you?

"Probably not."

Born in Binghamton, NY, **John M. Kuharik** is a 1971 Rider College graduate, an Army veteran, and a career public health retiree. He loves alternate universes, and time travel, and spends ridiculous amounts of time playing fantasy MMORG's. His stories, "Brainboy," "Don't See How It Won't Get Worse," and "Suddenly Tired," have appeared in *The Prairie Light Review*. Other Buckthorn Borough adventures appear in *The Digest Enthusiast* No. 2 and 4.

EQMM & AHMM at the Expo and Banquet

Mystery Games have become very popular in China, along with the TV series, *Star Detective*. This rising interest in mystery and detection has generated rising appreciation for stories there by masters like **Ellery Queen**, **John Dickson Carr**, and **Rex Stout**. The boom spawned the first International Murder Game Expo (IMG) held in Shanghai, in 2019. The event hosted **Martin Edwards**, **Soji Shimada**, and **Paul Halter**, who took part in the mystery games, along with the expo's consultant, **Fei Wu**. *EQMM* was well-represented there with a display, and **Janet Hutchings'** address to delegates via a prerecorded video.

The Wolfe Pack's fans of **Rex Stout's** Nero Wolfe sponsored, along with *AHMM*, their annual Black Orchid Novella Award on Dec. 7, 2019. **Linda Landrigan** presented the award to **Ted Burge** for his story "The Red Taxi." which will appear in the Jul/Aug 2020 issue of *AHMM*. Honorable mentions for the award were **Steve Liskow**, **Stephen D. Rogers**, and **Cynthia Roberts**.

Jeff Vorzimmer

Interviewed by Richard Krauss

"First appearing on newsstands in late 1952, *Manhunt* was the acknowledged successor to *Black Mask*, which had ceased publication the year before, as the venue for high-quality crime fiction."

–Excerpt from the back cover of *The Best of Manhunt* edited by Jeff Vorzimmer
Stark House Press, 2019

The Digest Enthusiast: What triggered the idea to publish *The Best of Manhunt*?

Jeff Vorzimmer: Otto Penzler. At the recent Bouchercon in Dallas Otto told me how much he liked the *Manhunt* anthology and I told him I had to publish it because he hadn't. It seemed that, after Otto published *The Black Lizard Big Book of Black Mask Stories* in 2010, a similar *Manhunt* anthology would have been a logical follow up, but eight years later he still hadn't done it, so I decided to step up and undertake it.

TDE: Your introduction to the book is terrific and answered a lot of the questions I had about the magazine's origins and its title. How did you unearth all this information?

JV: Fortunately there are quite a few of people who worked for the Scott Meredith Agency who are still around—Barry Malzberg, Larry Block and Henry Morrison—just to name three who contributed information about *Manhunt* and Scott Meredith's relationship to it.

Other sources of information were various biographies and interviews of people who worked with the publisher Archer St. John. One book that was a goldmine of information on the brothers St. John was

Front and back covers of *The Best of Manhunt* edited by Jeff Vorzimmer Stark House Press, 2019. The back cover shows the April 1957 issue of *Manhunt* which contains the infamous illustration by Jack Coughlin.

the excellent biography of Robert St. John, Archer's brother, *Merchant of Words*, by Terry Horowitz. Both brothers led fascinating lives.

I was also curious about the artist who did the now infamous "Object of Desire" illustration. Having had to do a bit of a detective work myself on this project, I decided to track down the artist. Once I realized that, if he were a young free-lance artist in the late-1950s, chances were pretty good that he would still be alive.

Since I had a scan of the illustration, I cropped the signature and saved it to a separate file and uploaded the image of the signature to Google Images and got several hits that identified the artist as Jack Coughlin, who was indeed still alive and still working at the age of 86. He had studied at the Rhode Island

School of Design and was currently Professor Emeritus at the University of Massachusetts Amherst. All in all, a well-respected artist who might not want to be reminded of a lawsuit that claimed he had drawn a pornographic image.

I managed to get in touch with him through an art gallery that sold his work. Coughlin and I emailed back and forth and then set up a phone interview. It wasn't so much that he wanted to forget the incident, but, rather, was surprised anyone still knew about it. He related the story to me with the same kind of detail you would expect of someone recalling events that had happened the day before.

His recollection was, one day when he was at St. John Publishing, the Art Director Charles Adams called him into his office. Adams

handed Coughlin a copy of the latest issue of *Manhunt* and asked him to turn to page 25, saying there was a problem with the illustration there and asked him to explain. Coughlin looked at it and naturally focused his attention on the woman in the illustration, and said he couldn't see a problem. Adams told him to look at the man in the illustration, specifically the man's crotch. It was then, what appeared to be a penis, almost leaped off the page. "Once you see it, you can't *not* see it," Coughlin said, laughing.

Coughlin insisted, of course, that it was a fluke created by the scratchboard engraving process of the *Manhunt* illustrations. Apparently someone at the printing plant in New Hampshire had noticed it and called Adams attention to it. St. John's was being sued over this issue Adams told Coughlin. We're going to need you before a judge for a disposition. Although state charges were dropped, Federal charges were pursued and Jack Coughlin's deposition was used in the defense of that case, but to no avail.

Eventually the Federal District's laundry list of objectionable matter in the April 1957 issue of *Manhunt* was reduced to just the Coughlin illustration and a story by Day Keene's son, Al James (Hjertstedt),

titled "Body on a White Carpet." On appeal a Federal judge upheld the original verdict and a fine of $5,000 for publisher Michael St. John (Archer's son). This would be the equivalent today of $43,000 dollars.

Jack Coughlin said he was summarily dismissed that day and was never asked to do another illustration for *Manhunt*. He confessed to having never known how the Federal court case played out other than the fact that charges against the Art Director, Charles Adams, had been dropped.

I told him what he'd been waiting 57 years to find out.

TDE: A subset of your new volume is actually a reprint of the earlier *Best of Manhunt* from Perma Books in 1958. Why did you decide to go this route?

JV: You couldn't do a "Best of" anthology of *Manhunt* without including all the stories in that 1958 anthology. On the other hand, the

stories included in that collection were only from the first four and half years of the magazine. So, I intended this to be an expanded edition of that first anthology. I also added three stories from the *Bloodhound* anthology, which itself, was an expanded edition of *The Best from Manhunt*.

It would also make it easier for those readers who *had* read Perma's *The Best from Manhunt* to skip over those stories, which appear in the same sequence as that anthology. That way they wouldn't have to figure which of the stories they'd read previously.

There are actually two subsets contained within the anthology. The first 16 stories appeared in the *Bloodhound Anthology* published in England the following year, 1959. *Bloodhound* was the British version of *Manhunt*.

Some of the criticism I received on the book noted that a third of the book reprinted the contents of the first *Manhunt* collection, but I would have had to include all those stories in any "best of" collection. Many of the other stories are making their first appearance in print since they were first published in the 1950s.

TDE: What were some of the challenges you overcame to create the collection?

JV: Ha! Where do I start? I guess the two biggest hurdles were tracking down information on a magazine about which little information exists and had ceased publication over fifty years ago. Similarly, was the problem of tracking down the estates of the authors, all of whom, but one, are dead.

I eventually was able to piece together the history of *Manhunt* from many different sources and a lot of detective work went into tracking down the estates, particularly those authors whose appearance in *Manhunt* seemed to be their only works of fiction. Two authors come immediately to mind—James E. Cronin and Jonathan Lord.

The case of James Cronin, author of "The Man Who Found the Money," was a good example. I couldn't find any information on a fiction writer by that name. It was as if that story was the only fiction he ever wrote, which turned out to be the case.

There was no mention of a James Cronin in any compendium of mystery writers. There was no information on the internet. I talked to Barry Malzberg about it. Barry worked for Scott Meredith for quite a few years, but the name didn't mean anything to him. He suggested that the name might be a pseudonym, but I dismissed that idea. It just didn't sound like the kind of name someone would select as a pseudonym.

When I interviewed Henry Morrison who also worked for Scott Meredith during the time they edited *Manhunt* in-house, he didn't remember anything about him other than the fact that he vaguely remembered Norman Lloyd, a producer for Revue Studios, calling to secure the rights to a story that ran in *Manhunt* for *Alfred Hitchcock Presents*.

It wasn't a very well-kept secret that the magazine was pretty much a showcase for Meredith's stable of writers. Morrison pointed out that once the magazine became popular, writers would submit stories directly to St. John's Publishing and on occasion they would add the story themselves to the magazine.

Opening page to James E. Cronin's story in *Manhunt* February 1954

The problem was that producers would call the Scott Meredith Agency to acquire the broadcast rights. Morrison would have to stall them until he could track down the author, sign them and then make the deal with the studio.

Apparently, they had as much trouble tracking down James Cronin as I did. I was getting nowhere trying to find information on a writer by that name, when I had an epiphany. I thought— wait— maybe he wasn't actually a writer, or, at least someone who made a living as a writer.

I had been reading quite a bit about stylometrics, which is, ostensibly, about identifying authors by textual evidence from a sample of writing. The focus is on internal evidence contained within the writing when external evidence is lacking, but it's not limited to just writing style.

So I reread the story looking for clues as to what the author might be if not a professional writer. It's amazing how much you gloss over when doing a casual reading of a story. Reading through the story again I took note of the fact that the protagonist was A) a college professor and B) from St. Louis, Missouri. Okay, so, maybe the writer was a college professor from St. Louis.

I went to newspapers.com and searched St. Louis newspapers from the mid-1950s and found there was indeed a James Cronin, who was a professor at St. Louis University *and* he taught a creative writing workshop!

After half an hour of searching, I found this little blurb on the bottom of page 15E of the December 26, 1960 edition of *The St. Louis Globe-Democrat*:

For the Record: Script for "The Man Who Found the Money," the story scheduled on "Hitchcock Presents" tomorrow night, was written by Dr. James E. Cronin of St. Louis U.

Of course, I was only halfway there. Now that I knew who he was, I had to track down his heirs. Using a combination of newspapers.com and ancestry.com I was able to track down his daughter through three marriages, to Florida where she was retired. I got a phone number for her from one of those on-line directories and called her. I asked if she was professor James E. Cronin's daughter and she confirmed she was. I told her I wanted to reprint her father's story and before I could say another word, she said, "The Man Who Found the Money!—you know it was turned into an episode of *Alfred Hitchcock*

Presents?" Apparently it was the only story he had ever written.

TDE: If success is longevity, *Manhunt* was certainly one of the most successful digests on the newsstand. There were 114 issues over its 15-year run. What was your process for selecting the best stories?

JV: Excellent question. I thought the best place to start was Bill Pronzini, who, aside from having read every issue of *Manhunt*, as well as *owning* every issue of *Manhunt*, he himself, has edited nearly 100 anthologies himself. With an introduction through Barry Malzberg I was able to enlist his help. Bill graciously offered his expertise. I asked him to put together a list of stories as a starting point. I then discussed the selections with other mystery writers such as Lawrence Block and experts on certain authors, such as David Rachels.

I also realized early on, that most of the best stories in *Manhunt* were from the 1950s. Sometime in the early 1960s, Scott Meredith pretty much ended his relationship with St. John and only 33 new stories by Meredith authors appeared during the 1960s. In 1964, *Manhunt* was reprinting a lot of stories that originally appeared in the magazine in the 1950s, as many as three per issue.

TDE: You selected Lawrence Block to write the Foreword and Barry Malzberg to write the Afterword. At what point did you get them involved in the project?

JV: Actually having Larry Block do an introduction or foreword was Barry Malzberg's idea and it made sense since he was the only surviving author of those included in the anthology and, like Barry himself, had worked for Scott Meredith. Both

Larry and Barry were involved in the project almost from its inception. I worked with Barry Malzberg to secure the rights to many of the stories in the book and he put me in touch with Larry Block and Henry Morrison. Larry Block graciously agreed to do the foreword and Barry offered to do the afterward.

TDE: What are you working on now?

JV: Soon after the release of *The Best of Manhunt*, at the end of July, Stark House could tell they had a winner as far as sales go. Within the first two weeks, I had already made back the advances and reprint rights and the publisher at Stark House, Greg Shephard, was already asking for a follow-up volume.

I had quite a few stories left over from the first volume, which amounted to about half of another volume. There were some excellent stories on Bill Pronizini's list I didn't have room for, that could go into a *More of the Best of Manhunt*. I had no hesitation about the quality of stories beyond the 39 that appeared in the first volume. The number of great stories that appeared in *Manhunt*, is far from being exhausted. I'll most likely have the second anthology out by mid-year.

The next project after the *Manhunt* anthology was a collection of three Beacon books for Stark House titled, appropriately enough, *A Trio of Beacon Books*, which collects *Marijuana Girl* by N. R. DeMexico, *Call South 3300* by Orrie Hitt and *The Sex Cure* by Elaine Dorian and is available now. These are three hard-to-find paperbacks, which command prices as high as $1,000 for *Marijuana Girl* and $500 for *The Sex Cure*. Of

course, these books have back stories that create a demand for them, which I cover in the introduction.

Recently I've been working with my friend David Rachels to produce two volumes of unpublished Gil Brewer stories. The first, *Death is a Private Eye*, is out now and the second, *Die Once—Die Twice*, we just finished and will be out at the end of January (2020). He and I just started on a volume of two Gil Brewer titles—out of print for over 50 years—which will come out in July. I also produced a volume of two books by Orrie Hitt writing as Kay Addams, *Warped Desire* and *The Strangest Sin*, with James Reasoner—he and I are big fans of Orrie Hitt. That will be out by the end of the month (November 2019). All of the these books will be published by Stark House Press.

Opening Lines

Selections from digests featured in this edition.

"When I first came to Madame Selina from the Orphan Home, half starved and one step ahead of consumption, I took every new thing for gospel, even Aurelius, late Emperor of the Romans, who is Madame's contact in the spirit world."
"The Ghostly Fireman" by Janice Law
AHMM April 2015

"The girl at the mike had a husky voice that did things to the spine."
"Big Steal" by Frank Kane
Manhunt December 25, 1954

"Ash, black and desolate stretched out on both sides of the road. Uneven heaps extended as far as the eye could see—the dim ruins of buildings, cities, a civilization—a corroded planet of debris, wind-whipped black particles of bone and steel and concrete mixed together in an aimless mortar."
"Pay for the Printer" by Philip K. Dick
Satellite Science Fiction October 1956

"When, at fourteen, Don began to work at the Aredia Grocery, a whole new wonderful world opened up to him; and not the least of its delights was the sense of worldliness he rapidly acquired, a sophistication beyond his years, with its attendant pleasurable notion that he had already seen enough of life to disillusion him with a certain well-known institution."
"A Bachelor in the Making"
by Charles Jackson *Manhunt* Dec. 1954

"By a strange twist of circumstances—call them coincidences if you will, or by another name if you can see relentless Purpose working through all things—I have lately, and almost simultaneously, come into possession of two remarkable revelations concerning the mystery of the Woman in Red—the heroine of that most astounding tragedy of Monte Carlo—and they supply the threads to lead a thoughtful mind either to its complete solution or, perhaps, to a still mistier labyrinth within the borderland between flesh and spirit."
"Unmasked" by Muriel Campbell Dyar
Weird Tales Spring 1973

"Dad Fluger had burned the beans again and only by infinite charity could the biscuits be termed edible."
Wild Horse Lode" by Ernest Haycock
Short Stories A Man's Magazine June 1958

"Ken Dexter was on his way to murder his wife."
"Revenge at the TV Corral!" by J. de Jarnette Wilkes *Beyond Infinity* Nov-Dec 1967

"I sat at my desk, listening to this doll rage half across the office. Our detective bureau is like most others, and women when they come in or are brought in are often hysterical."
"The Velvet Fist" by Harry Whittington
Shell Scott Mystery Magazine May 1966

"The wet brain shambled up the Bowery at the half-lurching, half-shuffling gait that is peculiar to all wet brains."
"The Wet Brain" by David Alexander
Manhunt November 1954

"It was two o'clock in the afternoon in the middle of August and it was hot, mid-Manhattan hot."
Homicide Hotel by Joe Barry
Phantom Books No. 500 1951

"To Will Durkin is seemed to be the realization of a long-cherished dream—this return from town over a rutted road, equipped and ready for a cruel duel with another man's offspring."
"The Cottage" by Frank Belknap Long
Fantastic Universe September 1954

"One evening along about seven o'clock I am sitting in Mindy's restaurant putting on the gefillte fish, which is a dish I am very fond of, when in comes three parties from Brooklyn wearing caps as follows: Harry the Horse, Little Isadore and Spanish John."
"Butch Minds the Baby" by Damon Runyon
The Saint Detective Magazine Spring 1953

"I stood at the bottom of the hill, staring up at Angels Flight, the famous little funicular railway in the Bunker Hill section of Los Angeles that brought people from Hill Street up to Olive."
"Ghosts of Bunker Hill" by Paul D. Marks
Ellery Queen Mystery Magazine Dec. 2016

"British men, being more reserved than Americans, don't stare as openly at attractive women under ordinary circumstances."
"The Sheik of Araby Affair"
by Robert Hart Davis (Richard Deming)
The Girl From U.N.C.L.E. December 1966

"Shayne made him pick up the tab at the diner they stopped at south of Charlotte, which was when Marty finally realized how much trouble he was in."
"Long Drive Home" by Andrew Welsh-Huggins *Tough 2: Crime Stories* August 2019

"Buchanan Smith, town tamer, tied his weary horse to the hitchrail in front of Keeley's Emporium; going into the store, he found John Keeley alone, checking over a shipment of cotton print dresses."
"Town Tamer" by Frank Gruber
Zane Grey Western Magazine April 1970

"When Hilda inherited a thousand shares of Intercontinental stock from this great-uncle of hers, I knew that it was my big chance."
"Death of a Dream" by James Holding
Shell Scott Mystery Magazine February 1966

Advertiser's Index